LOVE IS CRUEL

13 STORIES

Books by Hilary Davidson

STANDALONE NOVELS
Blood Always Tells
Her Last Breath
Every Lie I Told

THE LILY MOORE SERIES
The Damage Done
The Next One to Fall
Evil in All Its Disguises

THE SHADOWS OF NEW YORK SERIES
One Small Sacrifice
Don't Look Down

SHORT STORIES
The Black Widow Club
Dangerous to Know
Love Is Cruel

LOVE IS CRUEL

13 STORIES

HILARY DAVIDSON

ISBN-13: 978-1-962722-01-8 (Paperback)
ISBN-13: 978-1-962722-00-1 (eBook)

Cover design by Damonza
Author photograph by Anna Ty Bergman.

"A Special Kind of Hell" first appeared in *Beat to a Pulp, Round Two*

"Cold Comfort" first appeared in *At Home in the Dark*

"The Siege" first appeared in *Ellery Queen's Mystery Magazine*

"Swan Song" first appeared in *Unloaded*

"Unforgiven" first appeared in *Murder A-Go-Go's*

"Answered Prayers" first appeared in *Ellery Queen's Mystery Magazine*

"Ladykiller" first appeared in *Crime Factory: The First Shift*

"Magpie" first appeared in *Thuglit*

"Good Bones" first appeared in *Crime Factory*

"Hungry Heart" first appeared in *Trouble in the Heartland: Crime Fiction Inspired by the Songs of Bruce Springsteen*

"A Hopeless Case" first appeared in *All Due Respect*

"The Barnacle" first appeared in *Criminal Element's Malfeasance Occasional*

"My Sweet Angel of Death" first appeared in *Ellery Queen's Mystery Magazine*

For my parents, John and Sheila Davidson,
with boundless appreciation and love

CONTENTS

Foreword   9

A Special Kind of Hell   11

Cold Comfort   26

The Siege   49

Swan Song   70

Unforgiven   85

Answered Prayers   101

Ladykiller   127

Magpie   136

Good Bones   153

Hungry Heart   175

A Hopeless Case   182

The Barnacle   196

My Sweet Angel of Death   215

FOREWORD

When I published my first short-story collection, *The Black Widow Club,* in 2015, I never thought about having a theme. There were just nine stories I'd written early on in my crime-fiction career that I pulled together, and all they had in common was that I'd authored them.

But, ten years later, with more than fifty short stories out in the world, I had some decisions to make this time around. I've published plenty of stories set in far-off destinations (remember, I used to be a travel writer), stories about dysfunctional families, and stories about betrayal. As I sifted through them, there was one bloody thread that connected many of my favorites: ultimately, they were stories about love, and the terrible things people will do for it and because of it.

When I started writing fiction, nothing intrigued me more than a character's motive for doing terrible things. I don't think most people do bad things simply because they're bad. There's usually a reason, an internal logic, that ticks away like a clock in a person's head. I realized at some point that committing the darkest of crimes was all about having a justification that made sense — if only to one person in the world. Because the road to hell is paved with good intentions, that justification is often rooted in something pure and good: love.

The thing is, as much as we celebrate it, love is a powerful — often irresistible — feeling, not a moral quality. There's a reason it's so frequently compared to a drug. We understand people acting out of love as having a positive impulse, but it can just as easily twist dark. Love can inspire great things, but it can also spark jealousy, rage, and revenge. It can twist your brains and your guts, making you do things you never dreamed of.

Sometimes, love is beautiful to behold.

But sometimes, love is cruel.

A SPECIAL KIND OF HELL

"You understand this isn't about sex, don't you, honey?"

Paige hated it when her husband called her *honey*. It sounded so insincere as it rolled off his tongue. She bit the soft tissue of the wall of her cheek to tamp down her anger. "Yes," she muttered.

"You're sure you're okay with this?"

"I've told you a hundred times. What more do you want from me, Derek?"

Her husband sighed and glanced around the bistro. It was late Tuesday afternoon and the place was empty except for the staff. Paige wondered what they thought of the fortyish couple refusing to relinquish their corner table. She caught their loaded looks as they set tables for the dinner crowd, murmuring subversively in Spanish.

"Dr. Shapiro says it's a bad idea for me to go through with it if you're not okay with it," Derek said.

She gulped her third glass of chardonnay. It was an amazing trick Derek had pulled on her, really. He was forcing her to give him permission to indulge a twisted fantasy. If she didn't do it, she was a bad wife. *A fetish needs an outlet,* Dr. Shapiro had told them when they'd gone for counseling. *You can't think them away. They need a channel so that you can have a satisfying life as a couple.*

Bullshit, Paige had thought at the time. She hadn't changed her mind about that. "I don't understand why you want a dominatrix to torture you." Her face flushed as the words gushed out.

"Dr. Shapiro explained it to you, didn't he, Paige?" He took a sip of club soda, then steepled his fingers, taking on the serious, steady demeanor he assumed in front of juries when speaking on behalf of his shady clients. "Every day, literally hundreds of people look to me to take care of them. My employees, my clients. Charities I support…"

"I'm the one who helps charities," Paige said.

"With my money." Derek's voice was even. "Our money, of course. But I'm the one who has to go out and earn it. I have so many people depending on me. Think of what the kids' schools cost."

That jolted Paige. Everything had seemed fine between her and Derek when the kids were at home. But then Derek had insisted on shipping them off to Swiss academies. Once it was just the two of them at home, minus the sunshine and cover the kids provided, Derek's darker desires had flourished like poisonous plants. "But you're the one who insisted…"

"I'm in control twenty-four seven, and it's exhausting. I'm not complaining about how I live my life, but I need a release," Derek went on. "You understand the dominatrix and I aren't going to have sex, right? That's why the dungeons are legal, by the way. No sex. You can legally hire someone to beat you with a whip, so long as there's no sexual contact."

Paige hated the way he slithered behind lawyerly arguments when discussing something personal. Did he really think that highlighting the technicalities of a morals law was going to make her comfortable with the fact her husband was going to go into a dark room with some leather-clad woman with a whip? Paige couldn't put her finger on the part that bothered her the most. Her personal trainer liked to talk about trigger points in the body, and

Paige felt that a bunch of hers were being hammered at the same time.

"I just don't understand…" Paige started to say, but Derek had already opened his wallet and dropped several bills on the table.

"This doesn't have to be a big deal, Paige, unless you make it one. This is about satisfying my needs."

"But what about *my* needs?"

He stood without answering that. "Look, my appointment's at three. I want to be on time."

He meant his session at the dungeon, of course. It didn't matter how she felt; he was going no matter what she said.

"Let me put you in the car." Derek took her elbow. That made her feel older suddenly, like someone's maiden auntie. "You've had a lot to drink."

"I can get to the car." She pushed him away.

Derek called his driver. Finally, the black town car turned the corner and double-parked in front of the bistro. Derek stepped off the curb and opened the door for her.

Paige started to get in. "Why did you tell me, Derek? Why didn't you just do it quietly? I probably never would've known."

Derek gave her that flat, broad smile that worked on juries. "I couldn't keep secrets from you, honey." He nudged her into the car and shut the door. When she turned to look at him, he was already on the sidewalk, his shoulders squared and his step swift, as if he couldn't wait to get where he was headed.

"Home, ma'am?" the driver asked.

"Yes, please." Paige sat back and rubbed her eyes. Had it really come to this? Seventeen years of marriage to a man who secretly craved dungeon paddlings? Whips and chains? A ball gag? Paige wasn't even completely certain of the nature of his cravings.

A couple of sessions at Dr. Shapiro's townhouse hadn't enlightened her about that. The doctor talked mostly about how trust is the most important thing in a relationship and how you have a responsibility to satisfy your partner, even if their desires don't match up with yours.

I've been doing that for years, Paige had said.

I'm sure you think you have, the shrink told her.

She wanted to tell him about the occasional threesomes Derek wanted. She'd gone along with that, even though she hated them. She didn't care about kissing another woman. Paige had friends who liked to think they were sexually liberated and open, and they'd sometimes say over cocktails how wonderful it would be to have a threesome. Only, it wasn't wonderful when you were the one who was shoved aside in bed. There was nothing more humiliating than sitting there, sweaty and wet, while your husband and a rented siren went at it beside you. Paige had never known what to do then. Play with herself and pretend she was enjoying the show? Derek wasn't looking at her anyway.

As the car went up Madison, she caught sight of a mannequin in a plate-glass window. It sported a corset rimmed with black lace, and slender ribbons of garters that secured sheer black stockings. It was like looking at a retro pin-up, one holding something red in her hand. The light changed and the car surged ahead.

"Stop!" Paige shouted. "Stop here!"

"What is it, ma'am?" The driver asked, pulling over.

"I need to see... something... wait here."

Paige's legs were wobbly on the sidewalk. In front of the window, she realized the mannequin was holding a red paddle. It looked like suede, and Paige reached out to touch it, swaying slightly as her nails tapped the glass. The paddle had a red heart

Hilary Davidson

cut out of it near the top; that missing piece dangled from a red cord attached to the handle.

Would the dominatrix Derek was seeing hit him with something like that? Maybe the woman even shopped at this store. That thought made Paige recoil, as if she were standing on enemy territory. She gulped for air before she opened the door, expecting scorn. But the saleswoman who greeted her smiled, apparently not unaccustomed to the sight of confused, middle-aged ladies on the Upper East Side.

"I want that paddle in the window," Paige blurted out.

"Of course. Would you prefer red, pink, or black?"

"It comes in different colors?" Paige's words came out quietly, as if she'd used up all the air in her lungs on that first outburst.

"Yes. We also have one with a crystal handle. Well, that's more like a riding crop, but…"

"I'll take them all."

"Would you like them gift-wrapped?"

Paige shook her head. The woman leaned closer. "If you want, I can bring them into the dressing room for you to inspect. And if there's anything you'd like to try on…"

"Yes! The whole outfit." Paige turned to study the mannequin again. If that was what Derek wanted, she'd give it to him.

The saleswoman led her to a pink-walled room with a giant three-way mirror and rosy lighting. She sized her up and returned with a series of lacy corsets and garters, then came back with gloves, boots, and paddles.

"I look ridiculous," Paige said.

"Don't be silly. You've got a great figure. Your arms are better than Michelle Obama's." Paige smiled at the compliment.

"Do you have any idea how many women come in here for exactly the same thing? The kitten-with-a-whip fantasy is huge in these parts."

"My husband would laugh if he saw me dressed like this."

"I promise you, he won't. You'll do just fine." The saleswoman handed her the black paddle. "When you get the boots on, you'll look like Catwoman."

It felt like a flyswatter in Paige's hand. "How hard can you hit someone with it?"

"Don't worry. These are all very safe."

"It isn't even close to Halloween," Paige tried to joke.

"Listen, putting on a costume might feel weird, but what's the alternative? Sending him to a dominatrix?" The saleswoman chuckled and patted Paige's shoulder, mistaking her look of panic for nerves.

Paige worked through her anxiety by playing with the toys at home, mock-swiping at the leather armchair Derek liked to read in. When she finally wound up and hit it with a pink paddle, it let out a dull thud. As the wine wore off, she felt foolish, and hid the toys in their bedroom closet. Then she took a pill and waited for the panic to subside. It receded a little, like the tide, but waves lapped at her, some brushing her skin and making her shiver.

When Derek came home that night, he had a bouquet of red roses with him.

"How did everything go?" Paige asked. Her question was oblique, even though it was only the two of them in the cavernous apartment.

"Great." Derek smiled. "It was great."

"That's good." Paige wished she could bite off her tongue as soon as she said the words. "Do you want to talk about it?"

"Not particularly. You know when you've fantasized about something for so long, and then you get to experience it, and it's even better than you hoped? It's hard to really describe that to another person."

Derek's voice was warm and smooth, but each word hit her like the smack of a paddle. *Great. Better. Than. You. Hoped.* She bit the inside of her cheek to keep from crying out.

"So, what did you do with your afternoon?" Derek asked.

"I went shopping."

"There's a surprise."

"I bought something you'll like."

"Really?"

"Wait here."

She went to the closet. She thought about putting on the corset and stockings and boots, but she'd need more wine to manage that. Instead, she took out the paddles, examining each before settling on the red. In her mind, the dominatrix wore all black; she didn't want to mimic that. She held the paddle behind her back and went to the living room. Derek had already poured himself a scotch and was checking email.

"Did you want to see?" Paige asked.

"See what?" He didn't look up.

"What I bought this afternoon."

She held out the paddle. He took it from her, and a slow, sly grin crept across his face. "Oh, Paige. I never would've thought you had it in you. Where did you find that?"

She'd been terrified he'd burst out laughing, and she suddenly felt relieved. "I thought you might want to try it." Her voice was shy, almost girlish.

"Sure, I would. Put out your hand."

She reached to take the paddle from him, but he pulled it back. "Don't you…?" Don't you want me to take it? Before she could choke the words out he turned her hand over and whacked her palm.

"How'd you like that?" he asked.

She was ready to burst into tears. Not because of the pain — really, it was about as harmful as the snap of an elastic band — but because she was so baffled. Wasn't this what he wanted? What was wrong with her?

"Well?" he prodded. "Did you like it?"

"Yes?"

"Good. What's for dinner?"

Afterwards, when Derek took a work call and left her cleaning up the remnants of the meal, she went to the closet, pulled out the toys and the corset and the accessories, and put them down the garbage chute.

Derek made another appointment with the dominatrix, then another, and another. Each time, he made sure Paige knew what he was up to. "No secrets. That's the most important thing to me," he said one evening, after a politician's fundraising dinner that he'd dragged her to. They were in the backseat of the town car. "Don't you agree, Paige?"

"Yes."

"You know what's special about us, Paige? We can tell each other everything. I don't have to hide who I am from you and you don't have to hide things from me."

She'd been drinking, which always made her a little bolder. "How long do you think you're going to see this dominatrix?"

He raised his eyebrows. "Why?"

"I just want to know."

"Does it bother you? I've been completely upfront with you, Paige. I'd think you could return the courtesy."

"The courtesy?"

"Of trusting me. You know what's going on. What more do you want?"

"I thought you'd get this... thing... out of your system. I didn't think it would just go on and on and on."

"Paige, you need to deal with your own issues."

"My issues?" Her voice was so loud the driver glanced at them in the rearview mirror.

"Shh! This is about your own insecurity, Paige. Maybe this is about you aging, and feeling unattractive because of that."

"Feeling... unattractive?" He'd struck a nerve that vibrated through her whole body. It wasn't about age though; these issues had run through their marriage, with Paige feeling less substantial with each passing year. Living with Derek had hollowed her out to the point that the exterior had become brittle and tough to maintain. It was like a fine building that was ruined inside; sooner or later, the façade would come crashing down.

That night, she couldn't sleep. Even though Derek lay beside her, she felt a bridge between them that she couldn't cross. She wanted to be close to him, to bring him over to her side, but she had no idea how to do that. It wasn't until the next morning that she realized there was one person who could help her.

She hesitated when she stepped out of the cab in front of Dr. Shapiro's Gramercy Park brownstone. She'd called ahead, so he was expecting her. A middle-aged redhead she took for his wife answered the door and ushered her into an anteroom filled with towering bookcases. When Dr. Shapiro finally appeared, she'd picked up an art book and was leafing through it.

"Waterhouse. Interesting choice." He was a round man with a bald head and owlish glasses. He skin was pale, as if the sun never touched his face, and as smooth as a baby's.

"Is that some kind of test, having these books here? What does choosing the Waterhouse say about me?"

"This isn't a Rorschach test, Paige. It's a book. But, if you want something to consider, show me the paintings that intrigued you."

Feeling faintly ridiculous, Paige turned to an image of a flame-haired woman in a long, gauzy dress; her face was turned away from the viewer and she peered into a gold box that she'd started to crack open.

"Psyche opening the golden box. Interesting. Any others?"

It was like being asked to pick a tarot card by a fortune teller, Paige realized. She'd gone through a phase, a couple of years back, when she'd seen plenty of those, until she'd gotten wise to their tricks: the vague statements that were really questions, the hushed, anguished expressions when they pulled certain cards, their way of reshaping statements that didn't fit. Paige flipped through the book and showed Dr. Shapiro a dark-haired woman in a bold red dress, sitting at a loom and staring out a window.

"I Am Half-Sick of Shadows, Said the Lady of Shalott," Dr. Shapiro read. "Fascinating."

"Oh, and this one." Paige opened the book to a bare-breasted, alabaster-skinned woman lying dead on the ground, with a Roman centurion and wailing people in the background. "St. Eulalia," she added, before he could read the name next to it.

Dr. Shapiro gave her a sour look, as if she'd spoiled his fun. "Highly symbolic. Let's go into my office." He led her to the room at the back of the townhouse. There was a walnut desk and a big chair behind it, and a couple of plush chairs that she and Derek had sat in when they visited.

He closed the door. "You said on the phone you needed to talk. I should explain that, while I don't have an ethical problem treating both you and your husband, I cannot tell you anything from his sessions or vice versa. Is that understood?"

She felt like slapping the smugness off his face. Given what he was charging for a fifty-minute appointment, she was sure he'd have taken a sewer rat on as a patient if it paid in cash. "Yes."

"Well then," he settled into his seat. "What would you like to talk about?"

Paige cleared her throat. "I'm still struggling with my husband's… fascination… with seeing a dominatrix."

"That's understandable. Is there a particular aspect of it that bothers you?"

"Aspect?"

"Do you think about the woman, or fear your husband gains more pleasure with her than with you, or…"

He went on suggesting scenarios. What Paige wanted to ask was why her husband didn't want her to dominate him. Did he think she was unattractive? Did he think her a prude? That was at the heart of what tortured her, but she couldn't give it voice. Instead, she burst into tears.

Dr. Shapiro set a box of tissues on the chair next to her, but he didn't interrupt. She was glad, though she realized what a mistake she'd made by coming to his office. He couldn't help. No one could.

"I should go."

"Paige, I understand this is difficult to talk about. May I make a suggestion? Go home, and think about your reaction when your husband told you he wanted to role play."

"Think about... what? Derek never told me he wanted to role play."

"But when he first spoke to you at home about his desire to be dominated, how did you respond?"

"He never brought the subject up. The first time I heard about it was in your office."

Dr. Shapiro frowned. "You mean to say that your husband never broached this subject with you first? You had no indication from him of his desires?"

"No." Hot shame flooded her face as she answered. The humiliation, being married to a man for seventeen years and not understanding the seamier sides of his mind, not even knowing it was there. "One day he said we needed to go to couples counseling here, with you. That's when he dropped that bomb."

"But he told me the story of what happened when he tried to talk to you about it..."

"That never happened."

She started to leave.

"Interesting," Dr. Shapiro said. "The games couples play with each other."

"This isn't a game. Not to me."

"Well, it may be to your husband."

When Paige went home that afternoon, she ran a hot bath and took a bottle of wine with her into the tub. Maybe she would drown, like the Lady of Shalott. Wait, was that how the lady had died? It was in the Arthurian legend, something about a boat, but she didn't really remember it, and the painting in the book had just shown the lady staring out the window, daydreaming about Lancelot.

My husband hates me, she thought. *He's playing some sick game with me, and I don't even know it.* Derek needled her all the time, in small ways that were hard to point out to other people. It was a special kind of hell she found herself alone in. It was almost as if he derived pleasure from torturing her. Sadist, she thought.

She sat bolt upright, splashing water out of the tub. Was that what this game was about? Watch how she reacted when he caused her pain, and see how deep the wound went?

Paige clambered out of the bath and wrapped a towel around her. In her bedroom, she cursed herself for throwing away the corset. It had actually been pretty. Instead, she pulled on a black bra and panties and zipped up a pair of black boots with kitten heels. Over that outfit went a beige raincoat she belted closed.

She took a taxi to midtown. Five o'clock. Derek would still be at his office for a while. The receptionist smiled and greeted her, but Paige ignored the woman. She had something to ask Derek, and she was chewing the inside of her mouth, to work up the nerve.

His door was open and she walked in, shutting it behind her. Derek's desk was an uncluttered glass showpiece. His framed diplomas were on the wall, along with photos of Derek with politicians and his more infamous clients. His civic awards and golf trophies dotted the office. It was a temple to self-congratulation.

Derek looked up from his laptop. "Well, this is a surprise."

"Why did you never ask me?" Paige demanded.

"Ask you what?"

"Ask me to act like a dominatrix, if that's what you wanted. You've never been shy telling me what you want!" She opened her coat, letting it drop to the floor. She moved so that she was right in front of his desk.

He closed the computer. "Oh, Paige, I was just sparing you from making a fool of yourself."

"How?"

"This isn't about costumes or accessories. If I asked you to dominate me, I'd have to stage-manage you through the whole process."

"Is that what you think of me?" Paige demanded. "That I'm weak?"

"You're a hopeless pushover."

"That's not true."

"It doesn't matter what I do, you don't say no."

"That's not true!"

"You're weak, Paige. You always have been."

Without thinking, she grabbed one of the trophies and swung it at him. The wooden base connected with the side of his head, and a seam of blood opened and dripped down his cheek. Derek stared at her, stunned into silence. She swung again but he ducked and reached for the phone. Paige grabbed its base and swung, connecting with his face. Derek made an awful yelping cry, dropping the phone and putting his hands to his face. "Stop it!" Blood oozed over his lips when he spoke.

"No."

Paige struck him again, bringing the phone down on top of his head, and he crashed into the desk, cracking the glass. She grabbed a wooden plaque and smashed it against the back of his neck. There was blood and glass everywhere, and Derek was on the floor, curled up like a baby, sobbing. She pounded him again and again, all the while thinking, *I hope you're enjoying this.*

COLD COMFORT

The artists at the Humphrey Funeral Home were miracle workers, but even they couldn't piece Abby Killingsworth's face back together. In life, she had a curious charisma that was immediately striking in spite of her flaws. It was powerful yet puzzling: her eyes were wide-set and her nose had a bump and her lips were so plump and ripe that they lent her a faintly cartoonish appearance. Yet, when observed together in their heart-shaped frame, a peculiar alchemy occurred that could render complete strangers mute.

Abby had been a great beauty in life. In death, she was a broken statue, mere fragments of cold marble. My own heart had cracked in sadness when I first laid eyes on her lifeless body. In the oasis of false comfort that was the Humphrey Funeral Home, with its piped-in violin music, I kept up my unperturbed façade by imagining that Abby was elsewhere.

"The casket will stay closed," her mother announced. It was the day before Abby's funeral, and we stood together in a viewing room at the Humphrey. It was preposterously grand, with a domed ceiling that spoke of aspirations to royal chapelhood. Janet Killingsworth had asked me to accompany her to provide moral support, since her husband had refused to leave the house since his daughter's death. "I don't want anyone seeing what that bastard did to her." She bit her lip. "I'm sorry, Father, I didn't mean to swear."

"Please don't worry about that." I struggled to come up with something meaningful to say, anything that could blunt the pain. "Abby is at peace now, you must concentrate on that."

"Oh, Father, I try to. But when I think of what that monster did to my baby…" Janet's voice cracked. I put my hand on her shoulder, and she rested her head on my chest.

"Why would God take my baby?" Janet sobbed.

Of all the questions asked of me since I'd joined the priesthood, this was the most perplexing. I had no answers, only the same platitudes I'd heard since I was a boy growing up in County Cork. "All I can promise is that there is meaning in everything. It is invisible to us, so we must trust the Lord in all things."

Janet inhaled sharply and shuddered. "There's one other thing," she said, pulling away. "I want you to perform an Absolution for Abby."

I stared at her. Absolution had been removed from the Funeral Mass before I was born. I'd only performed it a handful of times, in unusual circumstances.

"My daughter may have been… involved with a man," Janet said quietly.

"What?"

Janet read the shock in my face, and quickly added. "Abby was such a good girl, and I don't know if it really counts as an affair, because she was separated from her husband, but…"

"Why would you suspect such a thing?"

Janet wiped her eyes. "Abby was pregnant."

"What? Abby told you that?"

"No, Father. The police did. It came up in the autopsy." She choked on that last word.

"The child might've been her husband's," I pointed out.

"No. Abby didn't see Frank at all. She told me she didn't." Janet gazed at me. "What did Abby say to you?"

"It wasn't anything she said outright," I explained. "It was her attitude. Whenever I visited her in the past few weeks, she was in a much more forgiving frame of mind about Frank. She believed he was capable of change, I think." I was silent for a moment. "I saw vases of daisies in her suite a couple of times. I suppose I simply assumed that they were from Frank. That was the flower they used at their wedding."

"She seemed so happy, before she died," Janet said softly. "Glowing. Almost as if she were in love. That wasn't because of Frank. She didn't love him anymore. A mother knows these things."

"You haven't said anything about this, have you?" I asked. "It's not anyone's business, but of course people might wonder..."

"No. I don't want her good name ruined. There are people who might think what that bastard—her husband, I mean—did to her was justified."

"No one would ever think that."

"Some people are cruel, Father. Abby was a good girl, but she... she had her flaws."

"We all do," I told her, speaking softly but with a firmness I hoped would comfort her. "We are all flawed creatures, yet the Lord loves us nonetheless."

The visitation started at three that afternoon. I stayed for the first two hours, offering comfort when I could. Abby had been an only child, but she had relatives on three continents, so her parents planned two days of visitation before her funeral to allow everyone to arrive in time. I left at five o'clock, stopping by my office at the church, as it was only six blocks from the funeral home. To my surprise, my secretary, Millie Tamliss, was still at her desk. She was seventy-two years old, with white hair and faded blue eyes. Her bones were only slightly larger than a sparrow's, and she seemed to live on air. In the years since I'd come to the parish, I'd never observed her eating or drinking.

"Good evening, Father. How was it?"

"Very sad. So many people came by to pay their respects. No one can quite believe it."

"I still can't, myself. Poor girl. It's heartbreaking." She clicked open her black patent purse, extracted a tissue, and blew her nose. "Just so you know, Father, there's something wrong with the phone line. It's been ringing off the hook for the past hour, but no one's there when I answer."

"Technology. Never reliable when you need it to be." I resisted the urge to glance at my watch. Mildred normally left the office by four, or four-thirty at the latest. Whomever was calling wasn't expecting her to answer. "Thank you for staying so late. You didn't have to do that."

"I thought it would be best. On account of the gentleman."

"What gentleman?"

"He's in your office."

I glanced at my door, which was closed all but an inch. My stomach churned slightly. Before I could ask her anything else, Mildred was up on her spindly legs. "I'm off to pay my respects to the Killingsworths," she announced. "Good night, Father."

"Good night," I murmured, and turned to my office. It was six steps from Mildred's desk. When I opened the door, I found a tall man in a suit studying my bookcase. His head swiveled in my direction. His thin face was narrowed to such a sharp point, it looked as if it had once been caught in a door.

"Good evening, Father Byrne," he said. "I'm Detective Reed. We talked on the phone a couple times."

"Yes, of course," I said, recognizing his voice. "Have you brought Frank DeSilva into custody?"

Frank was Abby's estranged husband, the man who went to the small hotel where Abby was renting a room and beat her to death. There had never been any doubt about who had murdered Abby. Frank was on camera entering the hotel, then departing with blood on his weathered hands and white shirt.

Reed shook his head. "He's still in the wind. I need to ask you a few more questions."

He was alone, which surprised me. I'd thought police officers did everything in pairs, like creatures bound for Noah's Ark.

"Of course. Would you care for some tea?"

"No, thanks.

I sat at my desk, surreptitiously checking to see if anything had been moved. The screen of my computer was on, which meant he'd touched it, though it was stuck on the password screen. "How can I help you?" I asked.

Reed stayed on his feet. "We're having trouble getting a bead on Frank DeSilva. His parents are dead, and he's got no family in the area."

"I'm sorry, but I don't know his friends."

"That's okay. I'd like you to tell me about Abby's relationship with her husband."

"I'm the priest who married them." I took a breath. "I've known Abby since I came to this parish seven years ago. She was a teenager then, fifteen or sixteen. Frank, I only met two years ago, when they became engaged and came to me for pre-marital counselling." I stared at my hands. "I didn't know that he was abusive towards her, not back then. I'm not even sure that he was abusive at that time. From what Abby told me, he started beating her after they came home from their honeymoon." I frowned, remembering exactly what Abby had told me about it. "There was a sporting event on television, a rugby match or something like it. Frank wanted to watch it and Abby had promised they would have dinner with her parents. That was the first time he hit her."

"Football," the detective corrected me. "It was football."

"That's it. But since you already know the story, why ask me?"

"It's often helpful to get different perspectives on the same event," Reed said.

"I see. Well, I didn't know what had transpired at the time. Abby came to church on a regular basis, but Frank rarely showed up. Christmas and Easter, those were the only times I saw him the year after they married. Then Abby suddenly left him. Her family was upset. They're very conservative."

"Yes, I've met them, Father."

His mouth twisted on that last word, and he frowned. I knew he was raised a Catholic from the way he addressed me. Perhaps he'd been an altar boy once.

"Abby's parents asked me to speak with her," I continued. "'Talk sense into her,' that was how they put it. I did, but then…"

My mouth was suddenly dry. I could still remember Abby, standing in my office in the exact spot the detective stood now, pulling off the cardigan she wore despite the summer heat, revealing an angry pattern of tangled red scars on her shoulder. Frank shoved me against a hot stove because he lost money on a poker game, Abby had cried out to me. You're telling me that I should go back to the man who did this to me?

"What is it?" Reed prompted me.

"When I counseled Abby, she told me about her husband's abuse. She told me things that still make me feel sick inside." I exhaled sharply. "It is my duty to love all of God's children, but I was horrified by what Frank had done."

"Did she show you any evidence?"

"Excuse me?"

"Did she show you any evidence? Photographs, video, anything like that?"

I blinked at him. "I took Abby's word for the truth, Detective. She was deeply shaken by what her husband had done."

"I didn't mean to suggest that we don't believe she was abused," Reed clarified. "But Abby only reported the abuse to you and to her parents. We've been interviewing her friends, and none of them knew anything about it. She admitted to her best friend that Frank had problems with drinking and gambling. Nothing about the violence."

"Abby was an intensely private young woman," I said. "Honestly, I think she had trouble believing the violence happened. That sort of thing wasn't supposed to occur in her world."

"Her parents were glad that she could confide in you."

"When she told me, I suddenly understood why she'd had so many inexplicable accidents. I remember her coming to church with a cast on one wrist, and later, on crutches one time. It all made sense when she told me the truth."

"What happened after Abby left Frank?"

"She moved back into her parents' home. She wanted to finish her university degree, since she hadn't graduated. Unfortunately, Frank would show up on their doorstep, demanding to see Abby. I know he sent her flowers. He tried to win her back. Their courtship had been a whirlwind, and he tried to re-create that."

"Did Abby call it a whirlwind?"

"No. Janet—Abby's mother—used that word. She talked to me when the pre-marital counselling started. She was concerned about Abby getting involved too quickly."

"She had doubts about Frank?"

"Yes. She never liked him, but her primary concern was that the relationship was moving too fast, and that Abby always leapt before she looked. She made snap decisions, sometimes to her detriment." I sighed. "Abby chose to leave her parents' home because Frank wouldn't let her alone there. Her parents supported her. They didn't want Abby to be harassed."

"And that's how Abby ended up at the Griffin Hotel. Nice place, maybe on the old-fashioned side. How far is it from here, maybe a fifteen-minute walk?"

The phone on my desk started to ring. I gave it a sidelong glance, then turned my attention back to the detective.

"Aren't you going to get that?" he asked.

"Mildred said there was a problem with the phone," I murmured, but I picked it up. "Hello?" I said.

"Father, I'm so glad you answered," said the voice on the other end. "I need…"

"Hello?" I said again. "Detective, I believe there is a problem with this phone line." I hung up. "I'm sorry, where were we?"

"Why don't you tell me about Frank DeSilva. The Killingsworths told me that he came to see you."

"Yes. When Frank couldn't find Abby at her parents' home any longer, he decided to come here." I took a breath, remembering the first time Frank had shown up solo at my office.

He wore a well-cut dark suit and an expensive watch and cufflinks, but he reeked of desperation, and his eyes were dark and hollow. Please, Father, help me get my wife back. Help her come to her senses, he had begged me. "I offered him my counsel."

"Meaning what, exactly?"

"I told him he needed anger-management counselling and help with his gambling and his drinking," I said. "I told him flatly that his wife would never come back if he couldn't be a proper husband."

"You believed Abby should go back to him?" Reed asked.

"I believe in forgiveness," I told him. "I believe in redemption."

"You thought Abby should forgive her husband?"

"Yes, for her own peace of mind. But I didn't believe they could live together again unless Frank changed."

"Tell me about Frank's visit to your office the day that Abby died," he said.

"We spoke about this on the phone already."

"True, but even the smallest detail might help."

I steepled my fingers together, conjuring up the memory. Frank had looked well the last time I'd laid eyes on him. He'd lost some weight when he stopped drinking, and he had an aura of fragile, almost boyish, hope. "Frank cared a tremendous deal about appearances," I said. "He came in, dressed in his best, hair neatly cut and such. He believed he was ready to be reconciled with Abby. It had been six months since she left him. I counselled him on patience." I paused again, remembering how I'd congratulated Frank, only my words had made his face pale. I pushed the thought away. "Frank didn't like to be told he couldn't have something he wanted, right when he wanted it."

"Your secretary, Mildred Tamliss, told me you left Frank in your office for a few minutes, and then Frank came running out like the devil was after him."

I rocked back in my chair, genuinely startled that Millie would be so indiscreet. "I had some literature I wanted to give him about anger-management therapy. I asked him to pray while I went to retrieve it. When I came back, Frank was gone."

"Here's what I'm struggling with," Reed said. "After Frank DeSilva left your office, he went to his estranged wife's place and beat her to death. I want to understand how that happened. Something in your conversation must've set him off."

I frowned at that. "You want to blame me for what Frank did?"

"Of course not. But something happened."

I shook my head. "I understand that my telling Frank he couldn't have what he wanted upset him. I take responsibility for that. Perhaps I could have… said something different. Perhaps I should have been kinder. Frank believed that he had done enough work on himself and he was entitled to his reward, which was Abby. I attempted to explain to him that the world didn't work that way."

"Did you tell him where he could find Abby?"

"Of course not." I rose to my feet. "You're leaving out part of the story. Frank left my office and went to a bar. At least, that's what you said on the phone."

He ignored that. "Did you know that Abby Killingsworth was pregnant when she died?"

"Yes."

"She told you?"

"Her mother did, this morning."

Reed's jaw tightened. It was obvious that he was disappointed. He had hoped to shake me with the news, and he had failed.

Still, he didn't give up. "Who was the father of the child?"

"How could I possibly know that?"

"Well, Father, Abby was living at a hotel for the past four months, so she didn't have neighbors who could identify you, but the hotel staff certainly does."

I'd been well aware, from the way he watched me and his abrupt manner, that he disliked me. There it was, suddenly, the real reason for his poisonous suspicion. It rocked me inside, though I was determined not to show it on my face. How dare he make such an assumption about me? What possible grounds could he have for it?

"I visited Abby every week," I said. "I listened to her confession. I gave her communion. She was afraid to come to church, in case her husband might surprise her there."

"Surely there are other churches she could've gone to, Father. Yours wasn't the only one."

"Abby needed support at a difficult time in her life. I am a longtime friend of her family. I wasn't about to abandon her in her time of need."

"How devoted of you. Didn't you comfort her?"

"Not in the way you're suggesting."

Reed's mouth twitched up in a rough facsimile of a smile. "I wouldn't blame you, Father. This isn't like those sicko priests molesting children. It's not a crime if you had a relationship with Abby. You're a good-looking guy. What are you, thirty-nine? Forty?"

"It's time for you to leave," I said, as calmly as I could manage. "Have a good evening, Detective."

❖

The next morning, I went to see Bishop Calton. He was a man I knew well, one with a fondness for dachshunds and Tolstoy and gin, but this wasn't a social call. He kept me waiting for half an hour in his library, a grand wood-paneled room with a vaulted ceiling and a ladder stretching two stories up. I was so engrossed I didn't hear him enter.

"Every time you come here, I feel like you're measuring the curtains, Michael." Calton was a red-cheeked elf of a man with a cap of wild white hair that appeared impervious to combing.

"Good morning, Your Excellency. Thank you for seeing me on short notice."

"I have an appointment at noon, so let's keep this brief."

"We have a problem. His name is Detective William Reed."

"I don't know the name."

"He's investigating the murder of one of my parishioners," I explained. "A woman named Abby Killingsworth, who was murdered by her husband. It should be an open-and-shut case. She was murdered in a hotel. There's video evidence. DNA evidence."

"What a sad circumstance," the bishop murmured.

"He came to see me last night. In the course of our interview, he made some odious statements about priests. Or rather, sicko priests, as he called them."

The bishop's white eyebrows shot heavenwards in alarm. "What does child abuse have to do with this case?"

"Absolutely nothing. But his hatred of the Church was palpable," I said. "Abby and her family are very involved in the church. I have the sense that he's trying to blame the Church for what happened."

"That won't do," the bishop said. "Not at all. What did you say his name was again?"

"Detective William Reed."

"We don't have the pull we used to," the bishop said. "However, if this detective is making statements against the Church and clergy in the course of his investigation, he must be removed."

"I agree heartily," I said. It was always important to allow the bishop to claim credit for whatever idea you came to him with. I'd learned that some years earlier.

We spoke only briefly after that. I drove back to the parish house and parked the car. I retrieved the mail and noticed, amid the advertisements, a hand-addressed envelope with no return address. I tore it open and found a note on plain white paper, written in a childish block print and replete with misspellings.

I'm desparate, Father. I don't know whoelse to turn to. Call me.

There was a telephone number I didn't recognize underneath. I stared at it, then went into the house and burned the missive and its cover. I didn't want to speak with Frank again. I didn't want to listen to his confession and hear him sob. I didn't want to have him describe the gory details of what he'd done to his wife, and how it hadn't really been his fault, because the alcohol always clouded his judgment and made him lose control. He would find a way to blame everyone else for the terrible choices he'd made, and for committing a horrific act of murder. Now that Abby was gone, I wished that he would vanish as well. There was no comfort I could offer him. I dropped the little ash-heap into the kitchen garbage, wiped my eyes, and headed to the funeral home for the second day of Abby's visitation.

That evening, I found Detective Reed waiting at my doorstep of the parish house. He gave me his sardonic smile. "Evening, Father Byrne. I'm here to offer you an apology."

"I don't believe we have anything further to discuss."

"I'm sorry our conversation yesterday upset you so much that you ran to your bishop," he said.

"I hope you might reflect on what you said to me. Your efforts should be concentrated on finding Frank."

"I have been reflecting, Father. More than you can imagine."

His words were mild, but there was an undercurrent of a threat in them, lurking like a worm in an apple.

"Well, then, I hope that you'll reconsider your animus toward the Church," I said.

"My animus is towards people who abuse positions of trust," Reed said. "I'll be honest with you. I was abused by a priest when I was an altar boy. It was an awful secret I kept from my family for years. I felt that if I said a word, God would strike me down. Doesn't that sound crazy, Father? The victim of the crime is made to feel like the guilty one."

His words stopped me short. "I am truly sorry that happened to you. I know the Church used to sweep crimes under the carpet. That was a tragedy."

"Since I'm off the case now, it doesn't really matter," he said. "My lieutenant worried that my experience biased my thinking. He's probably right. This isn't a child-abuse case, but I know exactly how manipulative priests can be."

"Good night, Detective Reed."

"Oh, I almost forgot. I brought you a present."

I eyed him warily. "Excuse me?"

Reed handed me an unsealed white envelope. There were two sheets of paper inside. The one on top looked like a photograph of a torn sheet of hotel stationary, only the gold griffin at the top of the page was severed in two. I could make out Abby's handwriting clearly. *Reasons I Will Never Go Back to Frank,* it read.

He made my life hell
He is crazy and violent
My mother has always hated him
He has a gambling addiction
He drinks too much
I don't love him anymore

"Hold on," Reed said, pulling that page out of my hands and gingerly folding it into thirds. "That wasn't supposed to be in there. The other page is for you." He took the envelope from me and replaced the note. I recognized it, but felt no need to tell him that.

"That was a note Abby wrote," I said. "I recognize her handwriting."

"Yes, we found it in her suite. The bottom of the page was torn off."

I remembered exactly what Abby had written. The last line of that list was Because I love you. I tamped the memory down. The police would never find that slip of paper; it was already ash.

"Abby Killingsworth didn't have many paper books, but she had an electronic reader," Reed added. "That page you're holding has a list of the books she downloaded in the past six months."

I glanced at it, and my eye fell on a book entitled *Dilemma*. I couldn't help it; I flinched.

"She bought Father Cutié's book," Reed said quietly. "Isn't that interesting?"

Father Cutié was a cautionary tale in the priesthood. A rising star in the Church, he was photographed embracing a woman on a beach in Miami; he abandoned the Church for that woman, and married her. *Dilemma* bore the subtitle, *A Priest's Struggle With Faith and Love,* and it was popular, especially among those who believed that the Church needed reform. He had since become an Episcopalian priest, and a powerful advocate for allowing Catholic priests to marry.

As I stared at the page, I could hear Abby's voice in the back of my mind. You could become an Anglican priest, Michael, she had told me. You would still have a parish. Think how wonderful it would be. She had been such a little fool. She refused to understand that serving an audience of dull, careless Protestants had little allure next to the might and glamour of Rome. It wasn't even a consolation prize; after everything I'd sacrificed in my life, it would be a crushing failure. I had failed to live up to my vows a mere handful of times; I wasn't going to depart from the Church because of a rare misstep I'd made.

"Here's what I'm sure of," Reed said. "You weren't just Abby's priest. You ministered to her in other ways. Hell, you might even be the father of her child, Father." He leered at me. "Wouldn't that be a kick in the head? How about a DNA sample to prove me wrong?"

"I'm not going to listen to this nonsense," I said, but I felt faint. There was a pounding behind my eyes that wouldn't die down.

"I also know that it's not a coincidence that Frank DeSilva went to see you, then killed Abby that same day. What did you say to him that set him off, Father Byrne?"

I didn't answer him, stepping toward the front door, key in hand.

"Here's what I can't quite put together," Reed said. "If you told Frank DeSilva you were sleeping with his wife, he probably would've killed you. What did you say?"

"I'm not responsible for what Frank did," I said. "He made his own choices. If you were any sort of proper detective, you'd find him, instead of harassing me." I went into the parish house and locked the door. Reed finally walked away, but the pounding in my head remained.

I couldn't sleep that night. There was an echo of Abby's voice still in my head. *I have wonderful news, Michael,* she had told me. *Don't be upset. I'm pregnant.*

The news had run through my body like an electric current, paralyzing me, rooting me to the spot. It was as if the doors of paradise had suddenly swung closed in my face. I was a man, subject to weakness as any man might be, only the punishment for any transgression was so much worse.

All I'd been able to say to Abby in return had been, *Then you'll have to go back to Frank.* The look she gave me then was seared on my brain. It was a mix of fury and contempt.

I'll never go back to Frank, she insisted. *Never.*

Make a list of pros and cons, I had told her. *Truly think about it. Write it down.* I had handed her one of those notepads they left by the bedside in hotels, along with the ballpoint pen with the name of The Griffin embossed in silver on the side. *One page for reasons to leave Frank, one page for reasons to stay.*

This is ridiculous, Abby protested.

Try it, I insisted. *See what happens.*

No matter which way I tossed and turned, I couldn't find any peace. Finally, I gave up, getting out of bed while it was still dark out and reviewing the remarks I was going to make at Abby's funeral that day. I'd always been an early riser, but it was a habit the priesthood had enhanced and reinforced; you simply didn't rise in the Church if you had trouble getting up in the morning. There were all manner of difficulties one could have, but not that one. I had some tea and took a long, solitary walk around the neighborhood and to the park, determined to clear my mind. None of it really helped. No matter what I did, there was a heaviness in my chest when I thought of Abby.

Her funeral mass was at ten that morning. I arrived at the church at eight-thirty. Abby's parents walked in just before nine; Janet was ghostly pale, while Stewart's face was red. I embraced them each in turn, murmuring words of comfort.

"You'll say the Absolution?" Janet whispered to me, while her husband wandered up to his daughter's coffin. The polished mahogany box was closed. Flowers lined its surface and greenery cascaded down the sides, as if it were a garden in bloom.

"Of course," I promised her.

Waves of mourners flowed into the church as somber organ music played. The Killingsworths were a popular family, wealthy and attractive, the sort of people one never imagined tragedy befalling. There were friends and supporters who loved them, and loved Abby, but there were also vultures there to witness their sorrow. I noticed a lone police officer looking vaguely out of place in the sanctuary; presumably, he was there in case Frank made an appearance.

Just before the service was to begin, I noticed that Janet wasn't in the front pew. Her husband was slumped there, head bowed.

"Where's Janet?" I whispered to him.

Stewart barely lifted his head. "She went out for a smoke."

There was a small side door that led to the church offices, as well as a small, private garden. It was as far as one could get from the mourners, and I imagined that was where Janet had gone for privacy. I headed that way, the din of voices and organ music behind me. It was only when I opened the door that I saw there were two people in the garden. Frank was holding a knife against Janet's throat.

"You drove us apart!" Frank seethed.

They both turned to stare at me.

"Frank, my son," I said. "Please, put down that knife."

"She hated me, Father," Frank gulped. "You know she did. You saw the list."

Abby's list of reasons not to go back to him, he meant. Sandwiched between, He is crazy and violent and He has a gambling addiction, were the words, in Abby's loopy handwriting, My mother has always hated him.

"Frank, give me the knife," I pleaded. "You're a child of God, no matter what you've done. Let go of Janet."

"She broke us up," Frank was weeping now. "She made Abby leave me."

"You hurt Abby," I said, as gently as I could. "That's why she left, Frank. Not because of her mother. Because of what happened between the two of you."

"I love her," Frank wept brokenly. "I really did. I didn't mean to hurt her…"

"Then let go of her mother," I insisted. "Let me help you, Frank. Give me the knife."

He shoved Janet away, and I caught her, but he held fast to the knife. Once I made sure Janet was steady, I asked her to step back and turned my attention to Frank.

"Give me the knife," I said. "We don't want anyone else getting hurt."

"Abby was everything to me," Frank whispered. "I didn't mean to kill her. After you told me she was pregnant…"

"I know, Frank, I know," I said softly. "You'll be reunited with her one day, I promise you."

"But… she's dead."

"She's moved into the next life," I whispered. "One day, so will you."

"But I'll go to hell, Father," Frank whispered back.

"There is no hell, except the one we make for ourselves. Now give me that knife. I'm afraid you'll use it to see Abby right now."

Frank gazed at me like a child in wonderment, fully understanding what I meant. He held the tip of the blade against his abdomen, as if deciding how to proceed.

"Damn you," Janet hissed, stepping forward and plunging the knife into his bowels. "Damn you to hell."

❖

The headlines died down within a fortnight, but I kept a few of the best in my study. My favorite was *Hero Priest Saves Grieving Mother From Daughter's Killer,* which was gloriously lurid. I sent it to my mother in Cork, expecting that she would be impressed, but her note of reply only mentioned that it should be Heroic. Hero or heroic, I would take it either way. Bishop Calton may not have cared much for me, but he'd had no choice but to nominate me for the title of monsignor. Rome no longer seemed like such a distant dream.

I attended Frank DeSilva's funeral, but no one else did. The police took no interest in his death. Janet and I both described it as a suicide, and they accepted that.

It was a surprise to have Detective Reed appear at my office at the church one morning, shortly after I arrived. He let out a low whistle at the sight of a framed cover from a local newspaper.

"My secretary insisted on doing that," I said, feeling my face redden.

"It's great publicity." He turned to face me. "But I wanted to give you a heads-up that you need to brace for some bad publicity."

"How's that?"

"I'd always wondered how you engineered everything," Reed said. "Abby's murder, specifically. It wasn't easy for me to piece it all together."

"Frank killed Abby. You know that. I had nothing to do with it."

"You had everything to do with it, Father," he said. "You had an affair with Abby. Please don't try to deny it. We know."

"Even if that were true—and it isn't—it has nothing to do with her death."

"It led directly to her death. You remember this piece of paper?" Reed pulled out the photocopy of Abby's list of reasons to leave Frank. "There are three sets of fingerprints on it. Abby's. Frank's. And yours."

"That proves nothing. I was the one who suggested to Abby that she write the list. I must've touched the page."

"You're the one who gave it to Frank," Reed said. "Because Frank had it after he left your office, when he hit the bar. The bartender remembers him mooning over it."

"You're suggesting I gave Frank that list. I didn't."

"Maybe you left it lying around your desk for him to find." Reed shrugged. "Maybe that's the reason you left him alone in your office. Give Frank some time to root around. How convenient that the name and address of the hotel Abby was staying in was at the top of the page."

"I can't believe you're spouting such nonsense." I tried to rise to my feet, but my legs were trembling. "You can't prove any of this."

"Here's something I can prove: the day Abby died, you called Frank and asked him to come to your office. We have the voicemail you left him."

I blinked at him silently. There was no answer for that.

"But you're right, it would be hard to prove all this in court," Reed said. "It's enough for me that I know the truth." He stepped toward to door. "And that Janet Killingsworth does too, of course."

"What are you doing? Filling Janet's head with lies?"

"Janet was deeply shaken by Frank's death at Abby's funeral. She had to be sedated for a few days. After that, we started talking. You know what she told me? Frank knew Abby was pregnant because you told him."

I swallowed hard. "What?"

"Janet remembers it very clearly. She was so upset at the time, with her daughter's funeral and thinking she was going to die herself, that she didn't put it all together. After we started comparing notes, she understood what had really happened to Abby. She knows you pulled Frank's strings. You gave him Abby's location."

"Frank made his own choices," I protested, but my voice was faint.

"You kept saying that," Reed observed. "But what I see, over and over, is you tempting others into sin, and evading consequences for it. But I don't think you'll be doing that much longer."

"Detective," I said urgently. "I have a confession to make. Frank didn't kill himself. Janet was the one who stabbed him."

Reed gazed at me, and his face cracked into a smile. "I know," he said.

I stared at him in astonishment. "Aren't you going to arrest her?"

"No, I'm not." Reed opened the door. "But I'd start making things right with my Maker, if I were you. I'd hate to guess how long you have to do it."

THE SIEGE

The red thong in my bed wasn't mine. It was curled up like a newborn rodent at the foot of the mattress, a lump with a tawdry tale to tell waiting for me when I came home from the Canyon Ranch spa in Arizona. When I found it, my six-month-old daughter, Sammie, was wailing from her crib. A cry threatened to burst out of my chest. I'd been away from home for a week, battling baby weight that wouldn't budge, and my husband was already having an affair.

I picked up the thong, holding it at arm's length for examination. The label was Victoria's Secret, and the size was extra-small. My husband always liked his girls petite. I knew that before I met him, back when I'd targeted him and plotted to meet him. Tony Salazar had that reputation. Everyone knew it.

Without thinking, I reached for a pair of scissors in my dresser and snipped the cheap lace into tiny bits. That little creature who'd crawled into my bed when I was away wasn't coming back, not if she wanted to live.

"Genie!" I shouted.

My maid appeared in the doorway a minute later. "Yes, Mrs. Salazar?" She gasped and her hand went to her chest. "Did you cut yourself?"

I looked down. The crimson dots of fabric looked like blood splatter on my white carpet.

"No!" I dropped the scissors on the bed. "Who's been in the house while I was away?"

Genie paled a little. "I don't think…"

"Who's been in here?"

Genie gulped. "No one I know of, Mrs. Salazar."

"I know someone else has been here!"

Her eyes were wide and fearful. "Not while I've been here, Mrs. Salazar."

That was the maid's way around it, of course. She was in the house from early in the morning until late at night, and she had a room in the house because she sometimes stayed overnight, but she didn't actually live with us. She shared an apartment with her elderly mother miles away in downtown Los Angeles. I knew from Genie's reaction that something was wrong, but I wouldn't be able to get it out of her at that moment. She'd worked for my husband for years, and her loyalty was to Tony.

"Clean up this mess," I said.

"Yes, Mrs. Salazar."

I brushed past her and walked down the hall. There was no point questioning Genie about the thong. It wasn't likely that Tony brought a girl over during the day. Whatever assignation he'd had had been at night, after the maid was gone. But there was someone else in the house who'd know if there'd been a secret guest.

I knocked on the door of my stepson's room. Jared opened it a moment later, his round, owlish eyes peering at me without blinking. He was small for an eleven year old, with a puny, sickly build that came from his mother's side of the family. She was another sparrow-boned creature who effortlessly maintained a size zero figure. I hated women like that.

"Hey, Jared," I gave him my brightest smile. It had won me a toothpaste commercial once, but it got no reaction from Jared.

"Hello, Cressida," he answered dutifully. "You're home."

He was an odd duck, an awkward, formal child who'd never been rude to me. Even so, he gave me the creeps. His head was always stuck in a book, and his cool, appraising gaze left me ill at ease. I was positive his scrawny mother was pouring poison into his ear about me. But I knew he didn't particularly care for her, either, since he'd asked to move into his father's house instead. Tony had his son during the week and his ex took the boy on weekends.

I was nervous about quizzing Jared, and I was well aware that I needed to win him over. "I brought you back something you'll like," I said. "I found it in this super-cute shop. It's still in my luggage, but Genie's unpacking that."

He blinked at me. Behind his glasses, his eyes looked huge. "Oh?"

"Toy soldiers. A set about the Alamo. I got you the church façade and everything."

Jared's thin mouth tightened in disapproval. "Did you know Sam Houston only sent Colonel Bowie to the Alamo to remove the artillery and destroy it? It was Colonel Neill who convinced him to defend it. The Battle of the Alamo never should have happened." He shook his head, making his mop of straw-colored hair fly around. "It is easier to find men who will volunteer to die, than to find those who are willing to endure pain with patience." He fixed his eyes on me again. "That's Julius Caesar."

"You really need a haircut, Jared." I looked inside his room. "Can I come in?"

He frowned, considering the question. I was dealing with the world's tiniest, most serious, sentry.

"I need to ask you something in private."

He nodded, then pulled the door back. "Okay."

Jared's room was at the back of the house, with a view of our gazebo and koi pond, but I doubted that he ever looked at them. The focal point was a giant table in the center of the room, which was covered with toy soldiers. My stepson might have been the only eleven-year-old in the word with a photo of General Patton hanging on his wall. There were busts of ancient Romans and Greeks on his desk, and more history books and maps than I could count. Jared was a nerd's nerd. All he cared about was ancient history.

"Wow, that looks cool," I lied, looking at the scene he'd set up on the big table. Armored toy soldiers were carefully planted over a molded landscape with a fort on a hill in the center and a pair of rivers painted on either side. "Are those Greek soldiers?"

"No, Roman. This is the siege of Alesia."

"I don't remember that from history class."

Jared raised his eyes to look at me. They were grey, like my husband's, with blue rimming the irises. "Did you ever read Julius Caesar's reports from Gaul? When you were in school, I mean."

"I was never a big reader," I admitted.

"Alesia was one of his greatest victories."

"Huh," I said. "It's so great you're into this stuff." I tried to figure how to approach the subject of his father's overnight guest. Obviously Jared's loyalty would be to his father, and I'd have to phrase my questions carefully to worm anything out of him.

"Caesar knew he could never win a full-frontal assault on Vercingetorix's fort," Jared said. "So he laid siege to it by building a wall so he could starve them out." He pointed at a ring of soldiers facing the fort, with a tall wall in front of them.

"They couldn't get past that wall, obviously," I said.

"No. Caesar built that wall. That's the circumvallation. It was to keep the troops in the fort stuck inside." He pointed at another ring of soldiers, further back and facing out. "That's the contravallation. It was another wall to keep the Gallic cavalry out, so they couldn't rescue the people inside." He gazed at it with a wonder that spanned the centuries. "It was genius."

"Look, Jared, I need to ask you something." I sat on the edge of his bed. It was neatly made, with corners folded with military precision. I didn't particularly like having him in the house, but at least he wasn't a slob. "How was everything last week, while I was gone?"

He frowned slightly. "Okay."

"Did you have any friends over?"

"No."

"What about your dad?"

Jared cocked his head to one side, like a bird. "What about him?"

"Did your dad have any friends over?"

Jared's eyes went cartoonishly wide, but he quickly turned away and started fussing with the toy soldiers. "Of course not." The words tumbled out of his mouth. It was painfully obvious to me that he was lying.

"It's okay, Jared. I don't mind. I was just curious because your dad's friend might've left something here."

Jared hunched his skinny shoulders in the biggest shrug he could manage. "Nobody visited." He paused, as if going through a mental register. "Nobody."

I smiled at him, even though I felt forlorn. I remembered the days when Tony and I met up while he was supposed to be working. He was a casting director with a full schedule that could open up at a minute's notice, if the mood struck him. That usually led to a hotel visit, but I wound up in his marital bed more than once, when his wife was away.

"Don't worry about it. It's okay," I told Jared.

He stared at me with his protruding, round eyes. I stood. "I'll see you at dinner."

"See you, Cressida."

I closed the door behind me. The kid knew more than he was telling. In a way, it didn't matter. Whatever bitch had been in the house wouldn't be coming back now that I was home. But if Tony was reverting to his old tricks, I needed to put up my guard. Maybe Jared had been trying to tell me something with those Roman walls. But I doubted that Julius Caesar could've built a wall that would keep Tony from straying.

I spent two hours combing my walk-in closet, searching for something to wear. Six months after giving birth was more than enough time to get into pre-baby shape, if you believed the Kardashians and the tabloids, but my thirty-five-year-old body hadn't bounced back the way I'd hoped. It was my own fault for snacking on anything other than ice cubes, but it wasn't easy trying to balance everything I had to do. I tried on several dresses and had to admit I looked a little lumpy. No wonder my husband was trawling for pint-sized flesh. By the time he arrived home, I'd poured myself into a wraparound number that showed off my breasts, which was the only part of my body that motherhood had improved.

"Hello, gorgeous," Tony said, sweeping me into his arms. "Sorry I couldn't get away sooner today. I missed you like crazy."

I'm sure you did, you lying, cheating creep, I thought. But what I said was, "I missed you, too, baby."

He let go of me quickly. "Where's the little cutie?" he asked. For whatever reason, Sammie didn't wail when daddy was around. That was a special torment she reserved for mommy.

Tony played with Sammie, cooing at her and telling her how perfect she was, until I got sick of listening to him and told Genie to give Sammie a bath and put her to bed. When I went into the dining room, Tony was deep in conversation with Jared. So much for my hopes of a romantic dinner.

"Life is a warfare and a stranger's sojourn, and after fame is oblivion," Jared recited.

"Marcus Aurelius." Tony nodded approvingly. "What else have they been teaching you?"

"We learned about Herostratus."

"Who's that?" I asked. I couldn't have cared less, but there was no other way to break into the conversation.

"He burned down the Temple of Artemis. It was one of the Seven Wonders of the ancient world, and he destroyed it," Jared answered. "Herostratus was sentenced to death, but he didn't care. He wanted everyone to know his name."

"Well, that's a stupid way to get famous," I said.

"It's easier to become famous for destroying something than for creating something," Tony said to me, like I was his kid instead of his wife. He turned to his son. "Did they teach you what else happened the night the Temple of Artemis was burned to the ground?"

"Alexander the Great was born." Jared didn't smile, but his face glowed with triumph. "It became part of the legend around him."

They went on like that through dinner, and I started to realize what was going on. Tony was avoiding me. I'd been away for a week, and he didn't seem to care. That brought me to the edge of panic. Whoever this chick was, she'd already gotten her claws into him. I'd assumed it was a one-time roll in the hay. But maybe there was more going on.

After dinner, I tried to talk to Tony. "I missed you so much when I was away," I said. "Did you miss me?"

"Of course I did, sweetheart."

He didn't sound very convincing. "Let's go upstairs," I suggested.

"Soon, baby. I've got some work to do first."

"Work? What kind of work do you have to do at..." I looked at my watch. "Ten-thirty at night?"

"Just a couple of emails. The director's in Europe right now and I've got to give her an update on a couple situations."

He vanished into his den. When he finally came upstairs, I was eating chocolate and watching a Lifetime movie.

"I thought you might be asleep by now," he said.

"I've been waiting for you." My voice was sullen.

"I figured you'd be exhausted after traveling."

The truth hit me suddenly: he'd deliberately been avoiding me. His guilt must've been getting to him. That wasn't the Tony I knew, the one who could have breakfast in bed with a girlfriend and then turn up at a family brunch with his wife and son.

"You're the best," he said, kissing the top of my head. But he didn't reach for me when he got into bed. Instead, he rolled over and went to sleep.

After that, things went back to normal for a few days, and I pushed my insecurities aside. No one knew better than I did that a casting director had women falling at their feet, day in and day out. I'd been one of those desperate actresses once, sending topless and naked "artistic" shots of myself around in the hope of landing a commercial or a bit part in a movie. I knew how the business worked, warts and all.

I knew I had to step up my post-pregnancy game, and I booked some sessions with a laser clinic that promised to drop you two dress sizes in a month. It sounded too good to be true, but I was desperate. I came home one day to find Genie standing in front of the house, staring at something she was holding. She didn't notice me until I slammed my car door.

"Hello, Mrs. Salazar." Her expression was guilty. "I'll put Mr. Salazar's mail in his study."

"Give it to me. I'll sort it."

Her expression showed me what she thought of that idea, but she handed the bundle of letters and catalogs over. What stood out was a fiery red envelope that matched the thong that had been hiding in my bed when I'd come home. Antonio Salazar was scrawled on the outside, with a tiny, incongruous heart dotting the I.

I didn't say anything to Genie. Instead, I stormed into the house and tore open the envelope. Printed on the front of card were the words, *You are my everything,* in elaborate gold calligraphy, with a pair of red and gold intertwined hearts underneath. Inside, a shaky hand had scrawled, *Love is composed of a single soul inhabiting two bodies.*

Each of the I's were dotted with a little heart.

My legs wobbled and I sank down onto the piled white carpet. What a fool I'd been. I'd believed Tony would be different with me than he'd been with his first wife. She'd let herself go completely after she'd had Jared, so it hadn't been hard to justify his waning interest in her. I knew I hadn't been his only girl on the side, not by a long shot. But then I'd gotten pregnant and made him leave his wife.

I stared at the remains of the red envelope. There was no return address, of course. There was a "forever" stamp, and the post office's mark canceling it was a black smudge.

There was a gentle cough, and I looked up to see Genie gazing at me with a concerned expression.

"Genie, have you ever seen an envelope like this before?"

"No, Mrs. Salazar."

She sounded sincere, but I didn't quite believe her.

"What is it?" I narrowed my eyes at her. "You know something, don't you?"

"No. I don't."

"Just spit it out."

"It's that... well, there are always ladies throwing themselves at Mr. Salazar, aren't there?" Her round face was earnest.

"Have you noticed anyone in particular?"

"No, Mrs. Salazar."

If Genie had been younger or more attractive, I would have suspected her. But she had a face that was more pleasant than pretty. She was very petite, but she was also six years older than me. It was hard to picture her throwing herself at Tony, and Tony not running away.

Calm down, I told myself. *It's a stupid card. It doesn't mean anything. It's not like anyone was in the house while I was out.* I felt a little better until I went upstairs to get an aspirin. In the bathroom of the master suite was a tube of lipstick that wasn't mine. It was inside the medicine cabinet, hanging out with the Advil and Claritin and Ambien and other pills we had. None of my makeup was in there. I picked the tube up. It was red. When I turned it over, I saw it was made by Rimmel. Who was this woman who was shopping at mall stores and coming on to my husband? I balanced the tube in my palm. Had it been in the medicine cabinet since I'd returned? I tried to remember if I'd opened the medicine cabinet, and I couldn't.

Either it had been sitting there for days, or Tony's new mistress had been inside the house while I was out.

That thought made me panic. I wouldn't go out again, I decided. Whoever this woman was, she was staking out her territory. It was a mind-game she was playing with me. I was certain that Tony had no idea what she was doing. He'd probably be horrified to learn what she was up to.

What a man will do with you, he'll do to you, my grandmother liked to say. It was Texas folk wisdom, but it had a ring of undeniable truth to it. My husband was cheating on me. I was going to have to put an end to it somehow. I didn't want to, but I knew I had to confront this problem head-on.

That night, when Tony got home, I dragged him upstairs to our bedroom and closed the door. Then I picked up the lipstick and presented it to him.

"What's this?" he asked, smiling. "It's not my color."

"It's not my color, either."

I stared at him until the mirth drained out of his face.

"I don't get it. Why are you showing me lipstick?"

"Why don't you tell me, Tony? Whose lipstick is it?"

His brow knit together. "Yours?"

"Wrong answer!"

He shrugged. "Come on, Cressida. You shop so much, you probably bought it last week and forgot about it."

My hand curled over the tube in a fist. "It's from a drugstore. Anyway, I'd never buy something this ugly."

"Maybe it was a gift with purchase?"

Something in me snapped at the mockery in his tone, and I threw the lipstick at him. It hit just under his left eye and he yelped.

"Who are you sleeping with?" I shouted.

"What is wrong with you?" he yelled back. "Are you a psycho? Knock it off."

My breath caught in my chest. *Georgina is such a psycho,* he always used to say when he was talking about his wife, before he left her. He never saw his own role in any of it, how he could drive a woman crazy with his obsessive womanizing. It would always be the woman's fault, and her responsibility. Tony saw himself as blameless. He was just playing around, after all. I hated him at that moment.

Sammie started crying, as if on cue. It was a welcome distraction, to go to her and try to comfort her, but my insides were roiling. For the rest of the evening, I managed to keep up a pretense that everything was fine, and Tony didn't say a word about our fight. But he hid out in his den for hours after dinner, so long that I lay down in bed and turned out the light. When I tried to sleep, acid crawled up my throat.

When he finally came to bed, I pretended to be unconscious. After a couple of minutes, he was snoring. The sound was too ridiculous to be faked. I got up and headed downstairs. The door of his den was locked, which only increased my suspicions. Where were his keys? I prowled through his jackets and came up empty. Returning to the bedroom, I crept around in the darkness, finally finding the keys in the pocket of his jeans.

I let myself into Tony's den, feeling like a defiant thief. What man locked up his home office from his wife? One so cautious that he'd built wall upon wall of defenses. It turned out

Hilary Davidson

that the lock on the door wasn't the only one. His computer was password-protected, and nothing I typed in unlocked it. His file cabinets were locked, too, and the keys weren't on the keychain. What kind of man hid puzzles inside puzzles? What was he so worried I'd find?

"What are you doing, Cressida?"

I turned and saw Jared. "Why aren't you in bed?" I demanded, angry that he'd snuck up on me.

"I heard someone downstairs and I thought…" His voice trailed off, and I realized he was holding a cell phone. He glanced down and pressed a single button. "I dialed 9-1-1 just in case it was a burglar, but I didn't press send."

"That was smart," I said feeling bad for scaring the kid. "Good thinking."

He gave me a slightly reproachful glance. "What are you doing in Dad's office?"

"I was just being silly, looking for something I gave him."

"Oh." He didn't look entirely convinced. "I'm going back to bed."

"Hey, Jared, will you do me a favor? Don't mention I was in here, okay?"

He nodded solemnly. "It's okay. Mom went through this, too."

"What do you mean?" I asked, suddenly alarmed.

"Mom says Dad can't be trusted," Jared whispered. "She hated that about him. She says he's always got somebody on the side."

That made me gulp. I'd been Tony's somebody-on-the-side for a while, but another woman had preceded me in that role, and another before her. Scratch the surface and you'd find a long line of women auditioning as Tony's love interest. The casting couch was a notorious cliché in the industry, but with good reason.

"Mom said it happened lots of times when they were married. Before I was born, even." Jared made one of his impassive shrugs. "She used to really hate him."

"Used to?"

"She's dating some guy now. Actually, she's engaged to him." The way he said engaged made it sound a step below murder. He rolled his owlish eyes for emphasis. "Yuck."

"You don't like him?" I'd had no idea Georgina was involved with anyone else, let alone planning to get married. It was a relief, not least because I could mentally cross her off my list of suspects. Georgina would hardly be sleeping with the ex-husband she hated when she was planning a wedding, now would she?

"He's stupid," Jared said bluntly. "He thinks that Russell Crowe movie Gladiator was real history."

"Wow, he's even dumber than me," I joked. But Jared nodded.

"He is."

Part of me wanted to throw something at the little jerk's retreating back as he padded up the stairs. But another part of me was crestfallen. Even Jared knew his father was cheating on me.

The next day was quiet, until the phone rang in the early evening. "Hello, is Tony there?" drawled a sweet, high-pitched voice.

"No, he isn't." Hairs rose up on the back of my neck. "Who is this?" I demanded.

She didn't answer my question. "Well, when will Tony be back?"

I hated the way she said *Toe-neeee*. She sounded young and kittenish, honey dripping from her stretched-out vowels.

"Listen to me, you little witch. Stay away from my husband."

She giggled then, long and loud like small child. "I don't think so," she said, before hanging up.

Her number was blocked, of course. I screamed and threw the phone against the wall. Only, it didn't hit the wall, but a mirror, which shattered into a thousand pieces. As is on cue, Sammie started bawling.

I wasn't sure how much more I could take. Then I caught sight of Tony in the doorway. He was carrying a bouquet of roses, but he was frowning. "What happened in here?"

"Nothing," I said.

He took in the broken mirror, and his mouth opened slightly but snapped shut again, as if he were about to speak but though better of it. Instead, he gave me a thin smile. "These are for you, baby."

All I could see when I gazed at the flowers was that the roses were pink, not red. Comfortable affection, not consuming passion. I didn't take them from him. "Give them to Genie. She can put them in a vase."

"Okay." He backed away from me. "It sounds like Sammie needs some attention. I'll get her."

He dropped the flowers on a sofa and backed out of the room. After he'd gone upstairs and Sammie's cried had subsided, I picked up the bouquet.

"He loves me, he loves me not," I recited, pulling petals off a rose and letting them fall to the carpet. Impatient, I started pulling off the heads of the roses. "He loves me, he loves me not, he loves me… he loves me not." The last of them was decapitated on the not. I dropped the empty stems back on the sofa and looked at my feet. Covered in rose petals, I might've been at a luxurious spa, trailing into a treatment room, following a trail of petals.

When Tony finally came back downstairs, his face was grim. "We need to talk, Cressida."

"It's dinnertime and Jared will be there," I pointed out.

"He's at a friend's house, working on a project for school." He paused. "You didn't know that?"

I shook my head. "He didn't tell me."

"It's on the kitchen calendar, Cressida." He pointed to the whiteboard. "See? You're not paying attention. It's like you're sleepwalking through life right now."

"I just had a baby! You can't…"

"You ignore Sammie." There was heat under his voice now. "I didn't think it was a great idea for you to go away for a week without her, but I held my tongue. But now I see you're a terrible mother."

"How dare you!" I shouted back. "You're a horrible husband! You're a cheat and a liar."

"What is wrong with you?"

"I'm married to a creep who starts cheating on me the second I turn around!"

"We're not having this conversation," Tony said. "Not with you like this."

"You're a monster. You ruined my life."

He put his hands up. "I know I'm not perfect. I never pretended I was. But I love my kids. I think you need help, Cressida. Professional help."

"You mean a psychiatrist."

"Well, if the shoe fits…" He cleared his throat. "Maybe a shrink would do you good. You've been erratic and irritable and… I don't know exactly, but you haven't been yourself."

"What does that even mean?"

"You're suspicious of everything, and you're angry all the time. Don't you remember when we used to have fun together?"

"Oh, I remember all right." What I remembered was this: when I'd met Tony, I was a model auditioning for a commercial his company was putting together. And after the standard audition, there was another, more private one, in a hotel room. "You're cheating on me."

"Cressida, I'm determined to be a good husband and a good father. I made a lot of mistakes with my first marriage, and I don't want to make them again. But you're making it impossible for me. You're kind of a lunatic."

"You're a fine one to talk," I shot back. "If I'm crazy, it's because you're making me crazy. You can't be trusted."

"You know what? I don't need to listen to this," Tony said. He turned on his heel and walked out of the house.

I lay awake for a long time that night, wondering what a psychiatrist would make of my brain. Then I wondered what one would make of my husband's. I slipped out of bed around five in the morning and went down to his den. I opened the file cabinet under the desk and my heart broke. It wasn't the manila folders stuffed with glossy photographs of stunning women, many of whom were topless, nude, or posed provocatively. It was the card that was pinned to his corkboard. I'd seen it before, but I'd never really noticed it. There was a photograph of a waterfall on the front. Handwritten on the inside were the words, "It is not death that a man should fear, but he should fear never beginning to live."

The I's weren't dotted with hearts, but the shaky handwriting was the same.

How long has this been going on? I wondered. I'd figured it was something that had come up while I'd been away at the spa. But that card had been there for ages. Whoever Tony was playing around with, it wasn't a new girl.

I grabbed a bunch of folders and stormed back upstairs to our bedroom. "Who is she?" I shouted at him, slamming the door and turning on the light.

Tony was a deep sleeper, so he was confused. He turned over and put his hand over his eyes. "What?"

I threw the folders in the air, so that photographs of nubile young women rained down around him. "What's her name?"

"Who?"

"The woman you're sleeping with now."

"We are not having this conversation. Especially not at…" He peeked at the digital clock. "Five-thirty in the morning. Have you lost your mind?"

"Is it her?" I picked up a glossy eight-by-ten photo of a blonde with an over-inflated chest.

"Stop it, Cressida."

I tried to rip the picture in half, but it was a heavy stock with a glossy coating that wouldn't tear. I grabbed the scissors from my dresser and hacked the blonde's head off.

"What about her?" I demanded, holding up a shot of a redhead with cascading hair like an old painting.

"Stop it."

"This one?" I didn't even look at the image, I just hacked another head off. "How about her?" Chop, chop.

"Okay, that's it." Tony sprinted out of bed. "I'm not going to put up with this. We need a break from each other." He grabbed his gym bag, dumped its contents onto the bed, and opened his closet. He grabbed a couple of shirts, but I wasn't really watching him. All I saw was a red envelope that had spilled out of the bag. I picked it up. On the front of the card was a cartoon drawing of a man and a woman. Inside, there was a single line of handwritten text. "What makes men indifferent to their wives is that they can see them when they please."

My hands shook. "What is this?"

He barely glanced at it, and he went right back to packing. "That's just a joke."

"A joke?"

"Not that you'd understand it," he said. "Because it's Ovid…"

He was still trying to explain it to me when I jammed the scissors into his neck. But I'd heard enough.

Jared came to see me in jail. The visitors' room wasn't much, just colorful plastic tables and chairs and hawk-eyed guards who hovered close by to listen in.

"You wanted to see me?" Jared asked.

"How's your dad?"

He perked up at that. "The doctors say he'll pull through. He'll be in the hospital for a couple of weeks, though. He almost died."

"If he'd died, Jared, it would've been your fault."

For the first time, he blinked. "Why do you say that?"

"You set this up." I swallowed hard. "From the start, it was all you. You played with your father and me as if we were those stupid toy soldiers of yours. You planted the thong, and the lipstick. You wrote those cards. I don't know who you got to call the house, but that was set up by you, too."

"Interesting theory," Jared said. "To be honest, I'm surprised you came up with it. What made you suspect me?"

"It was your dad. Right before I stabbed him, he said, Because's it's Ovid. At that moment, I didn't get it. Actually, I thought he might've said Olive. But no, the LAPD has the card in evidence, and it's Ovid. Which means it was you. No one but you goes around quoting old Greek guys."

"Ovid was a Roman, but I take your point." Jared nodded his head in a slow-motion bow at me. It felt like a sign of remote respect. "You're smarter than I thought, Cressida."

"But I still don't get it. Why would you do it?"

His eyes got rounder. "It's not clear?"

"I want to know why. Do you really hate me that much?"

Jared shook his head. "No. I don't hate you. It's my mom's fault."

"Georgina put you up to this?"

"No, of course not. My mom doesn't know. But she got engaged to that... ugh, that creep." For a second, Jared seemed like the eleven-year-old boy he was, instead of the ancient soul he normally channeled. "I hate him so much. He wants me to play baseball. He's nagging my mother about me all the time. I thought if... if you and my dad broke up, then my parents could get back together."

It was an eleven-year-old's logic, even if he'd taken inspiration from ancient warriors to accomplish his aim. "They're never getting back together, Jared."

His head drooped, and he took a deep breath. If I didn't know better, I thought he might be crying. "I know. Mom wouldn't even go to see Dad in the hospital. She told me…" He snuffled a bit. "She said she wished he'd died."

"I'm sorry, Jared." I meant it, too. "You can't manipulate people into wanting to be together."

"My dad won't press charges against you. I'll make sure of that." Jared took a handkerchief out of his pocket and blew his nose.

"Great. My life is a total disaster, but at least I won't spend it in jail."

"Who knows what will happen?" Jared stood up. "Do you know who Terence was?"

"No clue."

"He was a Roman playwright. He wrote, Where there's life, there's hope. Good luck, Cressida."

I sat there, as a guard let him out, turning the words over in my head. I'd lost the battle, that was true, but it was still too early to call the war.

SWAN SONG

It wasn't quite noon but Celina was on her third mimosa. I'd made them weaker than I would've for other guests, but that only made her gulp them down faster. "Alice," she stared at me intently. "If you were a man, would you want to fuck me?"

I glanced at the sunroom. My three-year-old twins, Aimee and Ava, were busy finger-painting something — hopefully paper — on the floor. They gave each other a curious little glance and went back to pretending to ignore us.

"You can't talk like that in front of the children," I whispered.

Celina took another drink, running one hand through her long platinum hair. She heaved a sigh, but her awe-inspiring chest barely deflated. When we were in our twenties, Celina's breasts had made her a favorite with Maxim magazine and earned her walk-on parts usually described in the script only as "the babe." Her agent had mined that hoary old trick, insuring her pneumatic assets with Lloyd's of London. A decade later, her chest was larger than ever, but no one in Hollywood seemed to care anymore. That didn't stop Celina from trying. On a quiet Sunday morning in New York, she had her extreme hourglass figure squeezed into a low-cut gold lame confection.

"Why are you asking?" I added, my voice still hushed. "You're not thinking of more surgery, are you?"

"Maybe I need to. It's not like I'm getting work. You know what I was offered on Thursday? Playing a mother on some lousy sitcom. I'm thirty-six and I'm not up for leading roles anymore." Her voice was getting louder. "The juicy, sexy parts are going to twenty-two-year-old airheads who are screwing anything with a fat wallet. No wonder Marilyn Monroe killed herself when she was thirty-six. Can you picture her playing someone's mother?"

"Mommy, we don't have orange." Aimee looked over. "We need orange."

"Daddy's going to bring orange paint with him when he comes home," I promised. "He said he'd pick it up." My husband was a specialist in rehabilitative medicine at New York Presbyterian Hospital. Sunday mornings were a busy time for him.

"We need it now," Ava yelled. "We need orange!" Turning three hadn't done away with the Terrible Twos. The twins were worse than ever.

"Why don't you mix red and yellow," I said. That earned me glares from the twins.

"Ugh, rugrats, you're giving Auntie Celina a headache." Celina's voice seeped through the room like poisonous gas. The twins settled back onto the floor, murmuring between themselves and casting furtive glances at Celina. They were fascinated by her, but never spoke to her directly.

I stood and walked into the sunroom, annoyed at Celina but unable to say so. She was so bitter these days that I could only take her presence in tiny draughts.

"Alice, where's that pitcher of mimosas?" called Celina.

"On the table," I answered, but as I glanced over, I saw that it was empty. Had Celina guzzled it down the second I'd moved away from my chair? I backtracked into the living room, picked up the pitcher, and went to the kitchen. Celina followed.

"It's so frustrating. I don't know what to do anymore," she whined. I wasn't about to press more oranges for fresh juice, so I extracted the ready-made kind from the fridge. "I'm no saint. I've slept with plenty of producers. But now, it's like I have to get on my knees just to get an audition for a shitty part I don't even want, you know?"

I poured champagne into the pitcher and stirred. "Mmm-hmm."

"I know I've got what it takes," Celina went on, pacing. "My acting coach says that she hasn't seen anyone since Cate Blanchett with talent like mine. She says the depths I can get to, the emotional honesty in my performances is just overwhelming. But how do I get to show that off? I don't have much time left if I'm going to be famous."

"It's getting harder out there all the time for actresses." I reached for the Grand Marnier. The mimosas needed just a splash. Maybe two.

"Easy for you to be smug. Not all of us can marry rich doctors and sit around all day doing nothing." Celina poured champagne directly into her glass. "Of course, I'm not saying you have it easy," she added slyly. "My grandmother always said that people who marry for money have to work hard to keep it. I wouldn't take on your life for anything."

"There's nothing I miss about Hollywood."

"You would've been a star if you stayed. But you threw it all away. For what? To be a house-mouse? This is your prize." Celina turned in a circle, lifting her hands at the stupidity of it all. My children, my husband, my Brooklyn brownstone, there was not one thing she could imagine wanting.

Sometimes it was hard to remember why Celina and I were still friends. I was fond of her when she was at her home in Los Angeles, but when she visited me, she grated on my nerves. She was my only connection to my former life as an actress. I'd met her when I'd first come to New York, a starry-eyed eighteen-year old who'd just taken her first plane ride. We'd been classmates at the Lee Strasberg Theatre and Film Institute and roommates at the Parkside Evangeline, the Gramercy Park residence for young single ladies that the Salvation Army used to run, before it sold the building for condos. Back then, Celina had awed me. She was just two years older, but I was from Battle Creek, Michigan, and she was the granddaughter of a Russian countess. "My family died in the Russian Revolution," she announced the day we met, speaking as dramatically as if her mother and father had just been shot by the Red Army, not four generations back. That it took me several years to even question her claim was perhaps a tribute to Celina's acting talent, or proof of what a rube I was.

"The problem with you, Alice, is you're a quitter," Celina said at lunch a week after our mimosa-fest. She'd disappeared for a few days, without telling me where, and now she was crackling with energy. "You could've been the next Naomi Watts. You could've had an Oscar! Instead you gave it all up to change diapers."

I took a bite of sea bass and tried not to grimace. Back in the day, I'd starred in a few plays so far off Broadway that the cast risked falling into the Hudson. I remembered years of auditioning when I was always hungry, partly because I had no money, but usually because I was starving myself for a role. Then I'd gone to Hollywood, and all I wanted to do was forget what had happened there. I forced my brain away from that unwelcome memory. It was a terrible time I'd never visit again.

"It's not like acting was the be-all of my existence. I was ready for a change," I said. "I was exhausted by trying to make it happen. Not the acting, but all the... other things." That was quite the euphemism, but I hoped Celina would pick up on what I was inferring.

"You didn't have what it takes to bask in the limelight. That's the bottom line. " Celina signaled to the waiter to bring her another glass of wine. I shook my head to indicate the round was only for her. "If you did, the desire would burn through you like a thousand stars. It would be the only thing that mattered."

"There are a lot of things that matter to me. That's not one of them."

"Well, I have news," Celina said. She stared at me, waiting for me to drag it out of her. "Because I have finally made it."

"Really?"

"You can't tell anyone this," she whispered. "But Edgar Ravovitch is casting me in his next film."

"The Hippopotamus?" My mouth went dry suddenly. Celina was smiling and nodding at me. The waiter put a fresh glass of white wine down in front of her and I turned my eyes toward him. "Actually, I'll have one of those, too, please."

"I knew I'd break you out of your little house-mouse rut," Celina said. "Cheers, sweetie."

Edgar Ravovitch had been making movies for thirty years. There were two rooms in his Hollywood Hills mansion devoted to the countless awards he'd won for writing, directing and producing. But there was another, more twisted accolade he'd earned over that time. He didn't just sexually exploit women, as so many film executives did; he humiliated and degraded them, and then he sometimes destroyed them.

"Celina, you can't be serious."

"I know, he's repulsive in every way. I don't think he's taken a shower in the past decade. He's so ginormous now he has to use one of those motorized scooters to get around. Imagine having your ass grabbed by that."

The waiter put a glass of wine in front of me and I drank half of it down in one gulp. It was clear that Celina had completely forgotten what had happened to me when I'd tangled with Edgar Ravovitch. That, or my friend was actually a far better actress than I'd ever realized.

"He's a dangerous man," I said.

"He's incredibly disgusting, but he makes stars. Look at his track record! This is the project that could put me over the top." She took another drink and shuddered. "And, Alice baby, I will have earned it. You have no idea."

"Please don't tell me you spent the past few days with him."

"He took me to Paris. Which I never really got to see, because those cobblestone streets are a bitch with a scooter." She rolled her eyes. "You're going to say that every girl sleeps with him for a part," Celina said. "That's true. That's how some of the most famous actresses in the world started out. He makes them famous. It's a trade." Celina finished the rest of her wine. "It's just business, after all. And that's how you do business with Edgar."

"There's no guarantee he'll do anything for you," I said.

"Of course he will." She narrowed her eyes at me. "Didn't he come through for you after your little interlude with him?"

I could feel my heart beating in my throat. She remembered, after all.

"Only somehow, you didn't have the nerve to go through with it. He offered you a starring role in that nineteenth-century hospital drama he made. You would've won an Oscar for sure." She peered at me with her fierce, feline eyes. "Maybe you were a little house-mouse then and just didn't realize it?"

Celina was, in many ways, the same woman I'd met at eighteen, only sharper around the edges, a diamond cut and faceted, smaller but undiminished, revealing more of the fire within. It was entirely possible that I was wrong to fear for her. She was stronger than I was, more determined. Bitterness had made her ruthless. It was quite possible she could deal with Edgar and win. I couldn't talk about what Edgar Ravovitch had done to me, so returned to her favorite subject.

"What's the film you'll be in?" My voice cracked on the question.

"It's a ghost story. You know that guy they're calling the new Brad Pitt? He's starring in it."

"And you are?"

"The movie is going to start with the scene where I get murdered. I'm an 18th-century English duchess. The costumes are going to be so beautiful!" Celina hugged herself quickly. "I know it's not a big part, but it's a prominent part, if you know what I mean. I have the weirdest feeling, like it's going to change my life. My psychic says it will. It's finally going to happen for me, Alice! I'm going to be famous, at last."

Celina returned to Hollywood for the filming. She sent me a purloined clip of the murder scene. It was brief but a showstopper, and my friend was the perfect icy goddess on celluloid. When she finally came back to New York, she was wearing a new ruby ring.

"You're not engaged?" I asked, horrified.

"No! It was a treat I bought myself, for all I've been through."

"Suffering for your art."

"More than you know," she answered. "Where's the champagne?"

Celina told me more than I wanted to know about Edgar while I watched my daughters playing in the sunroom. Their latest game seemed to involve barnyard animal noises, a blessing since they didn't hear a word of what Celina said. It was also darkly appropriate, given what she told me.

"You didn't," I gasped. "How could you stand it?"

"I kept thinking if it didn't kill Catherine the Great, it wouldn't kill me," Celina shuddered. "But it was horrific. It wasn't even a full-grown horse."

"How could you do it?"

"It takes a lot to impress Edgar. He gets bored easily." She stared at me. "Isn't that something like what he made you do?"

"No." I shook my head, pushing the memory as far from my consciousness as I could. "Not even close."

"He tied you up in his basement," Celina said, her eyes widening as she remembered the part of the story I'd been able to tell her.

I nodded slowly. "I thought I was going to die."

"Because of some light bondage?"

"It wasn't that. He opened up my veins. I thought I was going to bleed out."

Celina sat ramrod-straight. "I remember now. You were gone for days. I was worried about you! There were a couple of other blond actresses who went missing back then. I thought you'd be another one."

I closed my eyes, forcing back the tears. "It was torture," I whispered.

"That's grotesque," Celina said, slumping back. "No wonder you ran away from Hollywood."

I couldn't tell Celina the worst part of the story. I glanced at Ava and Aimee, who were engaged in a furious exchange of oinks. If any man ever did to them what Edgar Ravovitch had done to me, I would murder him. There wouldn't be a moment's hesitation. I wouldn't even feel a moment's guilt.

There was a long gulf of silence that opened between us.

"What I need to figure out now is what to wear to the premiere," said Celina, carrying the conversation over the terrible fault lines I'd opened up. She was oblivious to anything but herself, and I somehow found it endearing. A better friend might have pried. Celina didn't care enough to. "It's got to make a statement. It has to be memorable."

"Versace?"

Celina gave me a disapproving look that might've been a frown if she hadn't just been botoxed. "It can't be something a starlet would wear. It has to say that I have arrived. A star is born."

"Vintage Halston?"

Celina sighed. "I need to really cement myself in people's minds. Hardly anyone noticed Jennifer Lopez until she wore that dress cut down to her navel." She drank more champagne. "I need a dress that will make me famous."

The dress that Celina ultimately chose was breathtaking. She wouldn't tell me where she'd found it, or who the designer was, but it consisted of layer upon layer of sheer silk tulle with a peach body stocking underneath. There were hundreds of tiny, winking crystals sewn into the fabric, making the dress shimmer like a constellation on a summer night. On the night of the New York premiere, she got ready at my brownstone. The twins were at their grandparents' house in Queens so they wouldn't be underfoot. After her hairdresser and makeup artist left, Celina studied her reflection in the cheval mirror in my bedroom. "Seriously, Alice, what do you think?"

"You're like some impossible combination of Jayne Mansfield and Jean Harlow. Is that even possible? You look absolutely beautiful." She truly did. Her platinum hair and pale skin made her ethereal, and no one could help but stop and stare at that dress. While I was reassuring her, the doorbell rang.

"That'll be Harry Winston," Celina said, as if the jeweler's was a personal friend. "They're letting me borrow some diamonds. Earrings worth $50,000, or something like that." She beamed. "Just wait till I'm really famous. Then I'll get the good stuff. Necklaces worth millions." She stared at her reflection and smiled, as if envisioning her neck encircled by ropes of priceless stones. "They let you have anything you want when you're famous."

But it wasn't armed guards with jewelry, just a messenger with a note for me. I set it on the hall table and went back upstairs to Celina. Her cell phone rang. "My agent," she sighed before answering. "So where's my bouquet?" she said to him.

There was a pause. Then all Celina said was, "What?"

She was silent for a long time, her face frozen. Her eyes were wide as the first woman to be sacrificed in any horror movie.

"He can't do that. He can't I'll sue the bastard." She listened again, her teeth gritted. "Yes, I understand. Yes, I said I get it."

She shut the phone and threw it at my mirror, shattering the glass. "I'm going to kill that bastard!" she screamed.

"Celina, what...?"

"He cut me out of the movie. He replaced me with another actress."

"I'm so sorry," I said, and I meant it. This role was everything to Celina, and it had vanished. More than that, it was an opportunity for Edgar Ravovitch to demonstrate how cruel he could be on a whim. "Can you sue for breach of contract?"

Celina turned away and her voice was muffled. "Apparently it's all kosher with the contract. That bastard Edgar even made an extra payment. Hush money. The notation on it was Pony Express."

Her anguish and humiliation hit me in the chest. I went to hug her, but she pulled away. "I need to be alone, Alice."

I muttered a few words and left the room, feeling sorry for my friend, and hoping that this would be the push she needed to get out of a business that ate beautiful women alive.

The freshly delivered envelope was sitting on the hall table, where I'd dropped it. When I opened it, a blue piece of stationery fluttered out, curving through the air and landing at my feet.

It's such a shame, Alice. You would have been perfect for this role. Not the ghost, but the lead. If you'd stayed the course, you would have one at least one Oscar by now.

I recognized the handwriting, but even without that cue, I would've recognized the stench of Edgar Ravovitch anywhere. There was a heavy musk of sweat and blood desperation that hung around him like a shroud. It was in everything he touched. Suddenly, I was twenty-eight again, trapped in Edgar's basement dungeon for days. I'd thought I would die. Instead...

I rushed up the stairs. Celina was on the floor, sobbing as if her heart might break.

"How badly do you want to be famous?" I asked her.

She stared up at me. "You know I'd do anything."

"I can make it happen for you."

"Alice, have you lost your mind?" She made a strangled laugh through her tears "You're a Brooklyn house-mouse with two little rugrats. What on earth could you do?"

"I can give you exactly what you need. You can take my story and make it yours."

"I don't understand what you're saying."

"When I was trapped at Edgar Ravovitch's house, I wasn't the only actress in his dungeon. There was another girl there. Remember Contessa Kruzic?"

"Of course I do. That little witch stole a part right out from under me. I hated her." She stared at me, uncomprehending. "When she went missing, I felt kind of guilty, like maybe I'd caused it by hating her so much."

"Edgar had both of us tortured. He tied us up, starved us, and then had us both bled until we were weak as newborn kittens. Then he left us with nothing but a knife."

Celina's face went white as the ghost she'd played. "A knife?"

"He told us only one of us could leave the room alive. The one that did would star in his next film. Remember the one about the nineteenth-century nurse? The one that won five Oscars? That was the film." I sank to my knees in front of her. "I killed her, Celina. I crawled to the knife before she got to it. With the last bit of strength I had, I stabbed her in the leg. She'd already lost so much blood. She died quickly."

"You?" Celina breathed, her eyes fixed on mine. "You did that?"

"Not for the role. I didn't want to die." I stared at her, desperate. "Can you understand that? I just wanted to live. That's why I ran away afterwards. I didn't want fame after that."

"I thought Edgar was just a sexually exploitative freak…" she breathed.

"Edgar's sexual peccadilloes are just a little hobby on the side," I said. "His real lust is for blood. The actresses he's helped are the ones who came out of his little torture chamber. There are at least two others in freezers in his basement. He showed them to me when I was there. Mila Montgomery and Petra Jordan."

"Edgar killed them?"

"I think they were trapped in the same way I was. He has the girls kill each other, but the blood is all on his hands." I took a breath. "Look what he sent me tonight."

I handed her the note and watched her face morph from sorrow to rage. There was enough competition between us, even now, that the idea I could have been the leading lady in the film made her soul burn.

"That bastard," she seethed. "I really am going to murder him."

"That's exactly what I was thinking," I said. "Go to the premiere. Stick a knife into him. You'll be arrested, but when you are, you're going to tell the police what happened to you. How Edgar tortured you. How he killed other girls. How he's responsible for the death of Contessa Kruzic."

"But they'll blame me."

"You're the victim, Celina. You're like a hostage with Stockholm Syndrome. Edgar terrorized you to the point where you couldn't tell up from down, right from wrong."

Her tears were dry, and she was nodding. "I've been the victim, all this time." She was mentally preparing in the way we'd learned at the Lee Strasbourg School, internalizing a role until it rang true, until we were inseparable from it.

"Maybe he told you he wouldn't hurt other girls if you did what he said," I suggested. "I don't know. That's your part of the character to fill in. But the bottom line is, he's a monster and you're the one getting justice for all the women he's destroyed."

She nodded, now deep in thought, and got to her feet. "I need to fix my makeup," she said.

That night, Edgar Ravovitch's sensational murder dominated the news. The first headline I saw was, Larger-than-life director Edgar Ravovitch attacked by deranged diva at premiere.

It was a fortunate thing that the twins were staying at their grandparents' house. That meant I could stay up late, watching the news come in over a hundred different websites, each building a new detail on what that last one had. When my husband came home, he peered in at me, hunched over my laptop.

"What's so interesting, babe?" he asked, coming into the room and kissing the top of my head.

"There's a director, a monster who abused Celina for years. She finally struck back. Here, read this." I turned the computer so he could read the latest on TMZ, and I watched his face. He was so handsome, not at all like a leading man, but in a slightly rumpled, bespectacled way that made me feel safe.

"This is horrifying," he said. "Do you think it's all true?"

"They say the police have already gone to his home and found the bodies in freezers in his basement." My voice was shaky. "He made actresses literally fight to the death for starring roles in some of his films."

I could feel a shudder run through him. "That's insane. How could anyone…"

"I don't know," I said, standing to hug him. "I can't understand it. But I believe Celina. I know this guy is guilty. I've met him. He is evil personified." I took a couple of sharp breaths. "I'll have to testify for her in court. I don't want the girls dragged into anything, but I'll need to…"

"Don't worry about the girls. They're too young to understand whatever craziness Auntie Celina got herself into." He glanced at the screen again. "I'm so glad you left Lala-Land when you did, Alice. Those people are out of their heads." He kissed me again. "Do you want to stay up and talk?"

"Let's just go to bed. Give me a couple of minutes."

He left the room and I looked at the screen again. The front page of the New York Times had loaded again. There was a huge photograph of Celina at the preview, just after she'd been arrested. Her platinum hair fanned out around her like a halo, and her sheer dress made her look almost as naked as a Roman statue. But her face was the most mesmerizing thing of all. Her perfect features were in stark contrast with her haunted eyes, brimming with loss and sorrow. Avenging Angel, read the headline. Under it were the words Celina St. Cyr Slays Monster Who Murdered Missing Starlets.

In the space of a few hours, the director with the household name had fallen and a new star had arisen. I touched the screen, my index finger at the hollow of Celina's chiseled cheekbone.

"I always knew you'd be the famous one," I said, and closed the screen.

UNFORGIVEN

The day I found out my husband was dead, it broke my heart. But I collected enough of myself to drive into town and corner the sheriff for answers. The jail was around the corner from Main Street, a tidy rectangle of a building with a pair of Art Deco angels guarding the entrance. Back in the day, my little hometown had big dreams for itself; like my own, those had been crushed to dust.

"Cassie! I was just heading over to see you," the sheriff said when I walked in. That was an obvious lie. He was at his desk, with a spread from In-N-Out Burger laid in front of him.

I didn't waste any time. "I'm here about Ray."

The sheriff nodded and wiped his face with a napkin. He was red-faced and bulky, with a nose that had been broken a few times. It was hard to say if his face flushed, because he was always overheated. "You have no idea how sorry I am," he said.

"I heard he died in jail."

"Who told you that?"

"My father," I lied.

That earned a stiff little nod. "Okay. Yeah. We came back and found him in his cell. I feel terrible, Cassie. I wish I'd been able to stop him."

"Stop him?" I repeated, my voice flat.

"From killing himself," Steve explained. "You know... you know Ray killed himself, right?"

"He would never do that."

"I know it's hard to believe, Cassie. Your husband's been having issues lately. Drinking a lot. Maybe it was PTSD. So many guys in the service come back like that. Ray did, what, two full tours in Iraq, didn't he?"

I nodded.

"So, who's to say what kind of demons he brought home with him," the sheriff went on. "You never really know, do you?"

"I want to see Ray's body."

"That's not a good idea. Look, maybe you should talk to your dad. He's handling all the arrangements."

"Why would my dad do that?"

"Well, you're away so much, Cassie. And I guess everyone knows you and Ray were living separate lives. You can't hide much in a little town like Constantine."

I swallowed my anger, aware I needed to stay calm. My father controlled everything in our tiny town, including the sheriff. If I was ever going to get to the truth about what had happened, it wouldn't be by blowing up.

"How did Ray die?"

"He cut his wrists open. It was bad."

Automatically, I glanced in the direction of the town's single jail cell. It was pristine and empty. The acrid aroma of bleach hung in the air.

"How on earth did Ray get a knife into his cell?" I asked.

"He used a piece of metal he broke off the cot," the sheriff said. "We got rid of that cot first thing, of course. Damned dangerous to have it around."

He looked down at his rapidly cooling burger and fries, and I wondered if some part of him felt bad about lying to me. He wasn't an evil man, from what I knew, just an obedient one.

"There's one thing I just don't understand in all of this," I said. "Why did you arrest Ray in the first place?"

The sheriff shifted his bulk in his seat, and the chair squeaked under him. "He was drunk and disorderly. Screaming his head off. I only brought him in to calm him down. I figured he'd sleep it off."

"Are you saying it had nothing to do with Ray going over to my father's house?"

"How did you…" For the first time, the sheriff's weak chin quivered. "I mean, like I said, Ray was going bonkers, yelling and stuff. Your dad called me because he was worried about him. He told you about that?"

"No, he didn't," I answered. "But that doesn't matter. Like you said, you can't hide much in this little town."

Constantine wasn't the kind of place that came to mind when you heard California. It was far from the warm, balmy coast, caught between cheap land where oranges struggled to grow and the unforgiving heat of the desert. It existed in a strange time warp, where modern technology co-existed with strict 1950s values. It wasn't poor, exactly, but all its wealth was concentrated in the hands of one man, my father. You'd think that would give me a privileged perch, but I'd been trying to escape the town for most of my life. I'd believed that marrying Ray would finally let me leave, but Ray was snagged in my father's silvery web. He'd worked for my father and he'd ended up dead.

When I left the jail and got back into my car, I looked at my phone. There was the last message my husband had sent me:

Your father is a murderer. I'm going to make him pay for what he's done.

I hadn't seen the message until a couple of hours after he sent it, and then there was a long string of confused messages from me that Ray never answered.

What are you taking about?
What did he do?
Did you see him do it?
Are you okay?
Where are you?
Is this about my mother?

I read them over with a knot tightening in the pit of my stomach. The night before, I'd been furious with Ray for not answering me. It was only just dawning on me that he hadn't been able to.

Steeling myself for the worst, I drove to my father's house. It was a sprawling Victorian mansion that couldn't have been more out of place on the edge of the desert. No one answered the door when I knocked, which seemed unlikely. Part of me was relieved; I wasn't ready to confront my father. He had a way of making me feel as if I were being petulant and childish whenever I questioned him. The person I really wanted to see was my baby sister, Chloe. She was the one who'd called me that morning, just after I got home from my shift at a hospital in Long Beach. Her voice was barely a whisper. I overheard Dad this morning. He said Ray's dead. I don't know what happened, but Ray was here last night, freaking out. Dad had him arrested. Before I could formulate a question, she'd added, He'll kill me if he catches me with a phone. I'm so sorry, Cassie. The call was all of fifteen seconds long, but I knew Ray's death was a fact.

I couldn't call Chloe back; she'd undoubtedly borrowed her mother's cell to call me. My stepmother, Marielle, was a sweet woman, but she'd never been able to stand up to my father. She rarely left the house, and I had the uneasy feeling she was hiding in the shadowy hallway, holding her breath until I left. I didn't have a key; my father had never trusted me with one. Breaking in would get me nowhere. Instead, I left my car parked in the long driveway and crossed the road. There was a smaller house there, pretty like a gingerbread confection, where my older sister, Caron, lived with her husband and three children. When I knocked she answered the door with a wailing baby on one hip.

"Cassie. Oh, honey, I'm so sorry about Ray." She pulled me in for an awkward hug. "Are you okay?"

"No. The sheriff is trying to convince me that Ray killed himself and I know that's not true."

"He used something in the cell to cut his wrists. Dad told me this morning."

"Dad says a lot of things that aren't true," I said. "Can I come in?"

Caron's house was elegantly decorated with antique furniture, much like our father's was, but there were signs of kid-inspired chaos. Caron kicked a red truck under the piano bench. "Sorry the place is such a disaster. I have to get it cleaned before Mike gets home."

My sister was living the same life our mother had when we were young, before she'd vanished. I bit my tongue; we'd had too many arguments about her choice to live the life our father wanted for her and my decision to rebel. Truth was, neither option was working out well.

"I know you're busy," I said. "I just want to hear about what happened last night when Ray confronted Dad."

Caron shot me a pained look as she bounced the baby on her hip. "I don't know anything."

"You're right across the street. You must've heard something." When she didn't answer, I pulled out my phone. "Ray sent me this." I watched her face as she took it in.

"Why would Ray say that?" Her voice was soft. For a moment, I thought how incredible it was, that hearing someone call our father a murderer didn't make us blink an eyelash. "It doesn't make any sense," she went on. "He's always got along with Dad. Better than Mike does. Dad loves Ray because he was in the Army."

Caron's husband, Mike, was a nice enough guy, but he often came across as if he'd been dropped on his head when he was a kid, maybe more than once. He was the son of one of my father's business partners, so their pairing had been welcomed by my dad, but he didn't hide the fact he thought Mike was a dummy.

"Dad used to like Ray," I said. "But something's been off for a while. I don't know what happened."

"Didn't you ask?"

"I did, but…" My voice trailed off. "You know I've been working the night shift at a hospital, right?"

"The one you won't tell anyone the name of, so Dad can't get you fired?" Caron said.

My father hadn't minded me going to school to become a nurse, but it turned out that was because he wanted someone on call to help with his diabetes and arthritis. He didn't think a woman should have a job outside the home. I was twenty-eight years old and sneaking around just to work.

"The point is, Ray and I haven't been seeing much of each other," I admitted. "He didn't tell me what was going on. Except for that text. I think he knew something bad would happen to him if he confronted Dad." I took a deep breath. "Do you think Ray discovered something about Mom?"

"Stop it, Cassie." She was angry, which was how she reacted whenever I brought up the subject. "Dad didn't do anything to Mom. She left us. End of story."

"What kind of woman leaves her eight-year-old and ten-year-old and never contacts them again?" I asked. "I don't believe Dad. I never have."

"You've made that clear," she said. "Look, no one wants to believe their mother would leave them, but it happens every day."

"Would you leave your kids?" I challenged.

"Never." She glared at me and kissed the top of the baby's head. "Don't give me that look. Just because I wouldn't doesn't mean…"

"You know I can't let it go. I've looked for her, and she's nowhere to be found. Ray knew all about it. Maybe he figured something out…"

"This wasn't about Mom," Caron said. "Look, all I heard last night was one thing Ray shouted at Dad."

"What?"

"He was banging on the door, and he yelled, 'You murdered him, and I know how.'"

"Him?" I repeated. "You're sure Ray said him?"

"Positive. Dad opened the door and brought him into the house. After that," Caron paused, and she gazed at the baby, "I didn't see Ray again."

❖

I didn't confront my father until the day of Ray's funeral. The truth was, I could've gone over to his house at any time, but I wasn't ready to. I wanted to go through Ray's things, find whatever evidence he'd turned up, make my case from that. Only, there was nothing. Ray hadn't left behind so much as a suspicious matchbook. There were photographs and a handful of mementoes, mostly from Ray's tours of duty. He'd always liked to talk about his band of brothers, as he called them, and there he was, tanned dark and with shades on, grinning as they stood together in the sun; sometimes there were Iraqi coworkers in the group. There was nothing from Ray's childhood, but my husband had been orphaned young and shuttled through a series of foster homes. I knew he'd never cared to revisit those years. The Army was his real family.

On the day of Ray's funeral, I donned a black dress and drove myself to the church three blocks from the jail where Ray had died. It was the first time I'd laid eyes on my father since Ray's death. He was dressed in a dark suit that disguised some of his bulk, walking with a cane topped with a lion's head that was one of his more theatrical affectations.

"This is a nice turnout," my father said. "It's good to see so many people paying their respects."

"A lot of people miss Ray," I said.

"They're here for our family, Cassie." He nodded to himself, gazing at the crowd. "They're paying their respects to me. You know that."

It was all about him, as it always was. But I didn't care about his ardent narcissism that day. "What happened between you and Ray?" I asked. "You used to love him. Then something changed. What was it?"

My father's big shoulders made the slightest of shrugs. "He wasn't a good husband to you, Cassie. And believe it or not, family is all that matters to me. Nothing's more important that doing right by family. I know you don't want to hear it, but that's a fact."

"What are you saying? That Ray was cheating on me?" I shook my head. "Even when I was a kid, I knew you were cheating on Mom. You cheat on Marielle. You expect me to believe you would care if Ray cheated? To you, that's what a normal man does."

"In every part of life, there are rules you have to play by," he shot back.

"Like what?"

"Like stick to your own kind."

I stared at him as he walked away, my mind reeling. One of the things I'd loved about Ray was his open-mindedness about people. In some ways, he was a gun-toting, red-meat-eating conservative who fit into my father's world, but he was also a champion for Iraqis who'd helped US forces, and he'd helped several families settle in the US. You have no idea the risks those people took, working with us, Ray would say. There's nobody who hates terrorists more than they do. If Ray had fallen in love with one of those women, it wouldn't have shocked me. I'd married Ray to escape my father, not because I'd been in deeply in love. Ray was a good man, but we'd never really been on the same wavelength.

During the service, I wondered if the woman in question would show up. If she did, I didn't catch sight of her. But after the service, I went home and pulled out Ray's photos again. There were several with an Iraqi man and woman who were brother and sister. The man was called Mohammed; he'd worked as a translator. I stared at the woman with her dark hair mostly hidden by a headscarf and her shy smile. Samya, that was her name; I'd met her a couple of times. And I knew exactly where to find her.

The day after Ray's funeral, I escaped my family and drove west. I told myself all I wanted to see was the ocean, blue sky and water stretching into infinity on the horizon. But that wasn't true. Samya and her brother had settled into a little house in Murrieta. Finding it wasn't the hard part. What was a lot tougher was working up the nerve to knock on the door.

When Samya opened it we stared at each other for a breathless moment. She was barefoot, in jeans and a loose white cotton shirt. There was no headscarf today. Her lustrous black hair cascaded around her shoulders.

"Cassie," she said finally. "You're... Ray's wife."

"Sorry to drop in on you like this. If it's a bad time..."

"No, no. It is good to see you." Her dark eyes were filling with tears. "I am so sorry about Ray."

I hadn't been certain how she'd react to finding me on her doorstep. It had been at least six months since I'd seen her. She was thinner than I remembered, and I saw the dark half-moons under her eyes, the shadow over her delicate features. She was in mourning, of that I had no doubt. I had no idea how I was going to say what I needed to say to her.

"Where are my manners? Please, please, come in," she said.

I followed her, easy as a lamb. Her home was simply and sparsely furnished, which made it elegant. I'd been prepared for her to be angry or fearful, but her tenderness and sorrow disarmed me.

"I was just making tea," she said. "Let me pour you a cup."

Hilary Davidson

She did, but she didn't say another word. We slid into seats across from each other. "How have you been?" I asked.

"This has been the saddest time of my life," she answered softly. "Worse than that war. It feels like I have lost everything."

I stared at her. On the drive there, I'd been wondering how to broach the subject of her relationship with Ray. It hadn't occurred to me that she'd bring it up herself. You were sleeping with my husband, I wanted to say, but my mouth was parched. I took a sip of tea.

"Ray did so much for Mo and me," Samya continued. "He helped us come here, helped us get a place to live and furniture and work. He and Mo..." Her voice cracked and she started to sob. She choked out a few more words, but I couldn't understand them.

"I didn't realize you loved him," I said softly. "I'm so sorry."

Samya wiped her tears away, smearing her makeup. "I have been a mess since he died," she admitted. "I cannot eat. I cannot sleep. I keep seeing his face in front of my eyes. Only it was not his face anymore, because it was so broken."

"They... they let you see his body?"

Samya gulped and nodded. "I insisted. Because I knew he would never drive drunk. He would not drink at all."

I stared at her, realizing we were having two entirely separate conversations. "I don't understand," I said. "They told me Ray killed himself. That he cut his wrists..."

She shook her head. "I was talking about Mo. He died almost a month ago."

"Your brother..." The knowledge swept over me like a wave. I reached out for her hand. "I can't tell you how sorry I am. Please believe me. I didn't know."

"Ray didn't tell you?"

"We hadn't seen much of each other lately." That was an understatement. Our marriage had always been a long-distance affair, even when we were in the same room.

Samya looked down at her hands. "Ray and Mo were so close."

The knowledge landed like a gut punch, knocking the wind out of me, only it didn't hurt. Suddenly, I understood exactly what she meant. I'd been a little jealous about the idea of Ray being involved with another woman; on some ridiculous level, it made me feel like a failure. The fact that he was in love with a man meant it had nothing to do with me.

I took a deep breath. "Tell me how your brother died."

"The official story or the real one?" Samya asked, meeting my eyes again.

"Both."

"Officially, he drove his car off the road and it crashed in a ravine. They claim his blood alcohol was sky-high. But that's a lie. Mo never drank alcohol in his life." She pulled her arms around herself, as if suddenly chilled. "There were other things that were wrong. The car fell twenty feet. It wasn't smashed up. But Mo…" she took a breath. "He was so broken and bloody he didn't look like a person anymore. They said it was because he didn't have his seatbelt on. No. It was staged. All of it. I knew it and Ray knew it. Ray told me he was going to prove it."

"Did Ray tell you who did it?"

Samya gave me a long look, her dark eyes fearful.

"It was my father, wasn't it?"

She nodded. "Ray told me it wasn't the first time your father had someone killed that way."

Sunday dinner at my father's house was a longstanding family tradition. My stepmother, Marielle, cooked up a feast, as usual. There was pot roast and mashed potatoes, grilled root vegetables and heavy dressed salad. Midway through the meal, my father hoisted his glass of pinot noir in the air. "I don't suppose there's any reason to keep this secret any longer," he said. "To Chloe, who will be the most beautiful bride in the world this June."

There was silence around the table. "Charles, please," Marielle said. "You promised we would talk about this…"

"I've made up my mind," my father said. "It's in her best interest."

"Excuse me," Marielle whispered, getting up and rushing out of the room.

"She'll come around," my father said. "Women love nothing better than planning a wedding."

My sister Caron blanched. "But Chloe's sixteen."

"She'll be seventeen then," my father answered. "Chloe will be marrying the son of my good friend Glenn."

"Awesome! Glenn rocks," Caron's husband, Mike, leaned forward. "When we were in college, he was the kegger king."

Caron glanced at me. "Glenn Junior? But… isn't he thirty-four or -five? And divorced?"

"Which only means he'll be able to guide Chloe. That's what a girl needs. A good man to guide her."

"Amen to that!" Mike raised his glass and emptied it in a gulp. "Bitches be crazy without men to guide them. That's what I always say."

Caron shot me a look. Normally, I was the one who got upset with my father. Instead I raised my own glass. "Well, then. To Chloe and Glenn Junior."

I didn't even try to meet either of my sisters' eyes. Instead, I let my father prattle on, then asked about his gout. There was nothing he liked talking about more than his own health. I asked the occasional question but let him go on, not even commenting when he complained about his diabetes while consuming his second helping of apple pie a la mode.

After dinner, he asked me to look at his blood-sugar monitor and give him an injection. I knew he would; if there was one thing my father loved almost as much as throwing his weight around, it was being fussed over.

"These numbers aren't so good," I told him. That was the truth. "We should probably test your sugar level now, thanks to dinner and all that pie."

He sat calmly while I lanced his finger.

"You're not really going to marry Chloe off to Glenn Junior, are you?" I asked him. "Marielle seemed so sad. Chloe looked miserable about it."

"She's too young to know what's good for her. That's the problem with women: you give them choices, and they'll only make bad ones."

"Hmm, your blood sugar's through the roof right now," I said. "I'm going to give you a small shot of insulin, and we'll test again in a moment, okay?"

"Okay," he agreed.

I gave him the injection. "Of course, it's not only women who make bad choices."

He eyed me suspiciously. "Oh, really?"

"I'm sure you think Ray made bad decisions."

"That's true. At least, in one area. He was a good man. It's a shame what happened to him."

It was amazing to hear him speak about it, as if whatever happened to Ray didn't involve him in the slightest. That was the way it was with my father; I was never really going to get the answers I wanted from him.

"You really need to be more careful about what you eat," I told him, lancing the tip of another finger and giving him a second shot. "You don't make the best decisions for yourself."

"Of course I do." He was only mildly affronted. "But you're going to die of something one day. May as well enjoy yourself."

"Then it's a rational decision. A calculation."

"That's right. I weigh the options. Then I do the best I can for my family."

"Only things don't work out well for your family. Just for you."

His eyelids were fluttering now and he was sweating. "I don't feel right." His face was flushed and fearful. "What was in those shots?"

"Just your insulin," I told him. "Only they were very big shots."

"You're trying to kill me."

"No," I said softly. "Even though maybe you deserve that. I'm not a killer. But I'm not going to stand by and let you ruin more lives. You've done enough harm already."

"What's... what's happening to me?" he gasped. Sweat poured down his face.

"You're going into insulin shock. Give it a few minutes, and you'll be in a coma. You're going to stay in that coma for the rest of your life."

"Why?" he gasped. "Ray never even loved you."

"It's not just about Ray," I said, patting his arm. "You know that, don't you?"

"You won't get away with it."

"Yes, I will. I'm a nurse. And guess what? I'm doing what you wanted and quitting my job. I'm going to be devoting my time to your care, Dad."

His eyes were rolling up in their sockets.

"I know you killed Mom," I said. "Even though you'd never admit it."

"If I did… would you stop?"

"No, I'll never forgive you for that. Anyway, you'd just go on hurting people. It's all you know how to do."

He wasn't able to speak. His whole body was trembling. It was harder to watch than I'd expected. The prospect of losing control had always terrified my father. Now that it was actually happening, his face was a mask of terror.

"I don't want you to worry, Dad." I leaned in close. "You always said you did things for the good of our family. I promise you, I'll always try to do right by them." We'd never been affectionate with each other, but I reached out and held his hand until he slipped out of consciousness.

ANSWERED PRAYERS

"I've got a surprise for you," Mark said, leaning toward me across the table. In the warm candlelight of the restaurant, he looked like a movie star.

"A surprise?" I asked nervously. Lately, his passion for me had been cooling, and we'd seen less of each other. I'd been devastated at the thought he was losing interest, and I hadn't been sleeping well.

"Do you want to guess?"

"Did you get a new job? At a new magazine?"

He shook his head. "It's not about work. Not this time."

"Is... is your wife going away for a conference?" My voice was tentative. "So we'll be able to spend more time together?"

He smiled at me. "We will be spending a lot more time together, Carrie, but not because of any conference. I'm leaving my wife."

I watched Mark, waiting for him to burst my bubble. He'd said these words before, but they'd always been neutered when he added "next year" or "in a few months." We'd been dating for three years, during which my heart had seesawed up and down as my hopes rose and ebbed. I'd finally admitted to myself that he'd never leave his wife, that I was just like all the foolish lovers who believed a cheater's promise. Only it suddenly seemed that I had him all wrong.

"You're leaving Donatella? When?" My breath caught in my chest. Mark had been my boss once upon a time; in some ways, I'd never gotten over my heartsick crush on him. We'd been strictly professional while we worked together, but after I quit my job to freelance, things changed. When we started dating, I couldn't believe my luck, that a man like him—successful, smart, handsome—would be interested in me.

"I've already done it." His voice was proud.

Jumping out of my chair, I rushed into his arms. I was making a spectacle of myself in the middle of the restaurant, and I didn't even care. "This is the best news I could imagine."

He gave me his thousand-watt smile. "Not going to lie. I was hoping you'd be excited."

"You've been so distant lately. I thought you were going to dump me."

"Never. I just needed some space for my exit strategy."

When we went back to my condo that night, all I could think was that every dream I'd ever had about our relationship was coming true. When Mark left for work early in the morning, I lay in bed, half-dozing, wondering if this was some delicious but deceptive dream. My best friend, Jane, always insisted I was just Mark's piece on the side, and that he'd never leave his wealthy wife. She warned me that I was wasting my youth on a man who didn't really care for me, and even when I tuned her out, something in the tone of her voice made my biological clock start ticking in my ears. I was thirty-seven years old. It wasn't as if I were dying on the vine, but her words resonated even when I didn't want to hear them. It's high time you found a man who'll commit to you, she insisted. I couldn't wait to call her and tell her what had happened. Once she heard that Mark and I were together—truly together—maybe she'd be happy for me.

The door buzzer tore me out of my reverie. "Delivery," said a voice through the intercom.

In my dreamy state, I had an idea that Mark was sending me flowers, maybe a big bouquet of roses and lilies, to celebrate our newly official relationship. So I was taken aback to open the door and find a couple of burly men with a dozen large cardboard boxes.

"Carrie Barnes?" the taller one asked. "Where would you like us to put these?"

"What… what is this?"

"Delivery for you and a Mr. Mark Terrell." He pushed a tablet with an attached stylus into my hand. I signed reflexively.

"I guess you can put them in the living room," I said. "Where are the boxes from?"

"A Mrs. Mark Terrell." His knowing tone made me blush. I realized what had happened: in a fit of pique, Mark's wife—soon to be ex-wife—had boxed up his clothing and dumped it on me. It was a petty move, though she had every right to be angry.

I watched as the men piled the boxes up the walls. "We'll be back in a couple minutes," one called over his shoulder, halfway out the door.

"Why?"

"The rest of the boxes are still in the truck."

I watched helplessly as endless boxes filled the living room and the spare room I used as an office. Finally, they spilled into the bedroom. There were ninety-nine altogether, plus a couple of badly scuffed chairs and a ping-pong table that might've been stolen from a frat house. It took the men eight trips to bring everything up.

"This is the last one," the taller man said, handing a relatively small box to me. It was the robin's egg blue of a Tiffany box, maybe a foot-and-a-half square, but an envelope taped to the top obscured the store's logo. Carrie Barnes was scrawled on it, with the word Homewrecker underneath, as if that were my title.

After the men left, I brought the box into the bedroom, since there was nowhere else left to sit. Taking a deep breath, I pulled the envelope off and opened it.

Dear Homewrecker. The ink was burgundy-black, as if there were venom mixed in. *Congratulations, you win. I bet you're pretty pleased with yourself right now. I should've kicked Mark out a long time ago. I'm sick of your pathetic, psycho tricks. He's all yours!*

It wasn't signed, but there was a *PS* at the bottom of the page. *More tears are shed over answered prayers than unanswered ones. Enjoy him, while it lasts.*

I felt sick to the pit of my stomach. I opened the box slowly, afraid of what might be lurking within inside. I found shards of broken glass. Some pieces were large, with cut-crystal patterns on them. I reached for one, but another piece jabbed into my finger. I withdrew my hand as a drop of blood fell into the box. Shuddering, I felt as if a witch's curse had just been sealed.

When I tried to call Mark at work, I got his assistant instead. "He's in the middle of a meeting with the publisher," Alex told me. "It will probably be a while. Can I help you with anything?"

"It's a weird situation…" I bit my lip. I didn't know Alex that well, but I liked her. She was in her late twenties and from the Midwest, smart but self-deprecating, and she reminded me a little of myself when I first arrived in New York. "Did Mark say anything to you about his marriage?"

"Did he finally leave his wife?" Alex lowered her voice conspiratorially. "That woman is crazy."

"He did!" I let out a sigh of relief, glad to share the news. It really had happened. But a quick glance around the room showed me I had ninety-nine other problems. "The thing is, his wife just dumped all of his stuff at my place."

There was a stunned silence. "She... what?"

"A couple of delivery guys hauled tons of boxes over to my apartment. I don't know what to do."

"Sorry, I don't think I understood. Mark is living with you now?"

"I guess?" I answered, realizing that Mark and I really needed to talk.

"Wow, that was fast. Sorry, that came out wrong. Do you want me to come over and help with the boxes?" Alex offered.

"No, that's okay. Honestly, I think I'm mostly upset about the letter his wife sent to me. She called me a homewrecker."

"Seriously?" Alex asked. "That woman is unhinged. Be careful when you deal with her."

I spent the rest of the day trying to work, bumping into boxes whenever I got up from my desk. When Mark came in that night, I was sitting on the bed, knees pulled up to my chest, as if it were a life raft.

"Wow, that was no exaggeration about all the boxes." He gave a low whistle. "Donatella's nothing if not thorough."

"It looks like she packed up all your worldly possessions." I'd sent him some texts about the apartment after I'd talked to Alex, but I hadn't mentioned what was really eating at me.

"I'll have to get a storage unit. We can't live like this."

I nodded, realizing as he said it that—even though we hadn't discussed it—my condo was now our condo. I'd fantasized about us living together, but now that it had come to pass, I was numb. Part of it must've been the boxes. Part of it was definitely his wife's letter.

"Where should we grab dinner tonight?" Mark asked. He was a true Manhattanite in that he refused to eat anything at home but takeout. "While you think about it, I'll mix some drinks. I bought you champagne and St. Germain."

The first time Mark and I had gone out, we'd had champagne with a little bit of elderflower liqueur—better known as St. Germain—mixed in to sweeten it up. I was happy he remembered, but it didn't lessen my anxiety. "Mark, your wife sent me a weird letter."

I held out the envelope to him with a hand marked by a couple of band-aids. Mark opened the letter and shook his head. "I hoped Donatella wouldn't be bitter," he muttered.

"She has every right to be angry," I pointed out. I meant it. Even though I'd been having an affair with Mark, it had only started after he told me his marriage was over. How could I have known that wasn't true?

While Mark mixed the drinks, I chewed on my lip, working up the courage to ask the question that had haunted me all day. Finally, I just blurted it out. "Mark, did you choose to leave your wife, or did she dump you?"

Mark stared at me. "I can't believe those words just came out of your mouth, Carrie. Don't you trust me?"

"I do, but…" I took a deep breath. "In her letter, she says she kicked you out."

"That's technically true. When I told her I wanted to negotiate our divorce, she completely flipped out," he admitted. "I was planning to stay in our home for a while longer, especially while we figured out certain details. But Donatella had other ideas."

"Oh. I see."

"You don't sound convinced." There was a little twitch at the corner of one of Mark's eyes that left me uneasy. I'd seen it before, usually when the truth was being stretched particularly thin.

"It's just that…" I paused. "If you just told your wife you're leaving her, how did she pack your stuff up so quickly?"

"I bet she didn't sleep last night," he said quietly, looking around at the boxes. "She undoubtedly had her assistants helping her."

Donatella was an investment banker who had assistants at work as well as a personal assistant at home. It wasn't impossible to imagine a small army of worker bees packing all this up.

"It will be alright," Mark soothed me. "Just wait and see."

Even though I allowed myself to be lulled by him, it didn't escape my notice that he never asked about how I hurt my hand. I kept the broken crystal to myself.

If I thought living with Mark was going to be different from dating him, I was wrong. Dating, he never spent more than three nights a week at my condo; after he moved in, that rarely changed. As long as I'd known him, he spent every weekend in Massachusetts with his mother, who had made him promise she would live out her days in her own home even though she had Alzheimer's. I respected that about him, but it meant he was gone from Friday night or Saturday morning until Sunday evening.

The upside was that it was easy for me to make plans to see my friends. Jane and I had a standing date for brunch every Saturday. When I told her my news, she narrowed her eyes, cartoonishly skeptical.

"Did he get you a ring?" she demanded.

"Not yet."

"But you're living together?" Her eyebrows were raised so high it looked like they were stitched together.

"He just kind of automatically moved in," I admitted.

"Look, you know I'm not his biggest fan, right? So you'll have trouble hearing this because you think I'm biased. But it's not healthy for him to go straight from living off of his investment banker wife to living off of you. He's a parasite."

"That's not fair."

"What's not fair is this tick is sponging off you, Carrie. Don't be a doormat."

"Well, we are talking about marriage."

Jane scowled. "Well, it's time he put a ring on it."

"Tell me what's new with you."

Her face brightened suddenly. "I have news, too. I'm pregnant!"

My friend had gone through three rounds of IVF, and I couldn't have been happier for her. But I was also grateful for the distraction. When I told her that Mark and I had talked about marriage, it meant that I had brought up the subject, and Mark had shot me down. I'm not even divorced from Donatella yet, he'd said, rolling his eyes. It's going to be a long time before I get married again.

Even though I tried not to show it, his words made me panicky. Donatella's money had underwritten Mark's high-flying lifestyle. Mark was an editor at a celebrity magazine. It was a glamorous job filled with exciting parties and great perks, but it didn't pay well. Mark's casual dismissal of marriage made me wonder if I was a stepping stone between serious relationships.

That suspicion tormented me, but I soon realized I had much bigger problems. Ironically, they only hit after Mark's massive stack of boxes went into a storage unit. I'd had to find the space and pay for it; Mark's contribution was to send Alex over to help me ferry the boxes over in a series of trips. She was surprisingly cheerful about it.

"I'm sorry Mark made you do this," I told her late in the day. "It's unfair."

"It's no big deal." Alex's head was a halo of blond curls, and they spun around as she took in my apartment. "Your condo is beautiful," she added. "I couldn't even see it this morning thanks to all of Mark's boxes. This place is stunning. And now it's livable!"

She was right. Clearing out the boxes made the place feel like a home again, instead of a warehouse, and it allowed me to reclaim my office. As a freelance journalist, I didn't need much space to do my work, just a laptop and a phone. I'd tried to work around the mess, but I'd frequently ended up at the coffee shop down the block. That wasn't helping my productivity. It felt good to settle into my space again. But that feeling was short-lived, because of the small box that arrived the next day.

I carried it into my office and opened it without thinking twice. When I pulled up the top flap, I was mystified, because it looked like a black void at the bottom of the box... only that black void was moving. I screamed as I dropped the box. Cockroaches spilled onto the floor and scattered in all directions while I stood helplessly, my heart rattling in my chest. It was a scene from a horror movie. One bug shambled out of the box and onto my foot, and I shrieked as I shook it off and crushed it. A moment later, I remembered that you're never supposed to crush cockroaches, because their eggs will spray everywhere.

For a moment I stood there, staring back and forth at the bug and the box. Only then did I notice that Homewrecker was written in black marker on one of the box's flaps.

I ran out of the apartment and called Mark. "Your wife... your wife..." I gasped.

"What did Donatella do?"

"Bugs. Bugs everywhere." I couldn't stop shaking.

Mark came home early that day, finding me at the coffee shop at the end of the block. He went back to the apartment, packed an overnight bag for both of us, and checked us into a hotel.

"Are you sure there aren't bugs in there?" I asked him, for the hundredth time, once we were in the hotel room.

"I was careful, Carrie, I promise." He shook his head. "I'm so disappointed in Donatella. She's going over the edge."

Mark called an exterminator and arranged for the apartment to be sprayed the next day. "I feel bad asking this, since it's all my fault, but can we put this on your card, Carrie?" he asked me. "Mine's getting maxed out."

He wasn't joking about that. Two days later, when we were checking out of the hotel, his card was declined and I paid instead. Still, I was grateful to be back in my own home, and to have the roach problem taken care of. Or mostly taken care of. When I walked in, there's a roach on the bathroom floor, on its back, quivering in its death throes. I flushed it down the toilet and washed my hands. When I caught my pale reflection in the mirror, all I could think was that I'd brought this on myself. I prayed that Mark would leave his wife, and he had. Her rage was directed at me, and I'd earned it. I hoped knowing that she'd terrified me out of my own home would placate her. You won, she wrote in her note to me. But it felt like I was on the losing side. After what I'd done, I couldn't even defend myself.

Hilary Davidson

The ugly incidents piled up. They came at random intervals over the next several weeks. There was no pattern to them; they were as likely to happen on a Monday as a Friday. Some of them were simple, like the hairy red-brown tarantula that popped out of one small cardboard box (fortunately for me, the spider seemed to be startled out of a nap, and I was able to shove the box back over its quivering body until Mark came home and dealt with it). Others were more pointed. In the latter category was an email entitled "Homewrecker Carrie Barnes Porn Tape" that landed in my email inbox at four o'clock on a Friday afternoon. I watched five seconds of it in horror, realizing someone had manipulated the video, superimposing my face over the actress's. I slammed the computer shut, sickened and shaken.

Mark's ex has every right to hate you, I reminded myself. But how far was she going to push it?

Mark was sympathetic that night. "Donatella's crazy, you know that. Don't take it personally," he told me.

"She's trying to destroy my life."

"I don't know if this would help at all…" He paused, keeping his eyes on mine.

"What, Mark?"

"What would you think if we got engaged?"

My breath cut into my chest sharply. "I thought you didn't want to get married again?"

He smiled. "Donatella made me pretty cynical about marriage, but with you, it's different, Carrie."

In spite of everything that had happened, I was overjoyed. We kissed, but then Mark let go and reached for his briefcase. "I almost forgot…" he said. My eyes swam with tears. He'd bought me a ring already? I was so touched. But then he pulled a sheaf of papers out and handed them to me with a pen. "Just a formality," he said.

"Are you asking me to sign a pre-nup?" I was surprised. Mark owned next to nothing, besides a lot of clothes and a scuffed ping-pong table.

"It's a community property agreement," Mark said. "Because my divorce probably won't be finalized for quite a while."

"Oh," I said, starting to read it over.

"It's boring legalese," he said. "But it ensures that you get whatever I have, if I die. Or if I'm hospitalized, you make medical decisions for me. And vice versa, of course. Otherwise, my ex would be doing that." He nuzzled my neck. "And now you're my fiancée."

My hand shook with excitement as I signed. It felt like we were starting over, with a serious commitment between us. So I was surprised when Mark got up on Saturday morning and started packing for Massachusetts.

"Do you really have to go?" I asked him.

"To see my mother? Yes, obviously."

"I understand that. It's just... you go every single weekend." I stared at the floor, feeling ashamed of myself, even as the words tumbled out of my mouth. "Maybe I should come with you this weekend? I mean, after all, we're engaged now."

Mark raised an eyebrow. "Do you really think a patient with advanced Alzheimer's Disease is up for meeting new people?"

"If you think it's a problem, I don't have to meet her. I can stay out of the way."

"That's not going to work, Carrie. Obviously." He uttered that last word with such emphasis that I lost all dignity.

"You're never here for me! I barely see you any more than I did when you were still with your wife."

"You know how busy my schedule is, Carrie. I can't believe you're nagging me about this."

"It's wrong that you're gone every single weekend. There's no reason I couldn't go with you!"

"Do you think my mother needs to be bothered by someone in your emotional state?" he shot back. He picked up his weekend bag and walked out of the bedroom without another word.

I was devastated. Since Mark had moved in, our relationship had careened downhill, and no impromptu engagement could change that. I felt so sick that I even cancelled on Jane. I'm sorry, I can't make brunch today, I texted her, feeling like a heel.

Is this because of that stupid video? she shot back. Want me to come over?

The reminder of the fake video only made my mood darker. It hadn't just landed in my inbox; it was circulating far and wide. From the concerned texts and emails I'd read, few of the recipients were fooled into thinking it was me in the video (though one male editor I worked with commented, "Mark's a lucky man!!!"). But it was still humiliating. All I could do was shut off my phone and power down my laptop. At loose ends, I opened up Mark's briefcase and started to read the document I'd signed in haste the night before. It was generally what Mark had described, only most of the giving seemed to be on my side. My only real asset was the apartment, and Mark suddenly owned half of it.

Jane's words for him floated through my mind. Tick. Parasite. His ex had kicked him out and now he'd attached himself to me.

I was re-reading the agreement late that afternoon—feeling queasier by the minute—when I got a delivery from my local liquor store. There was a small bottle of St. Germain, that elderflower liqueur I loved, and a half-bottle of champagne. With it was a computer-printed note in the bag. *I'm sorry we fought this morning,* it said. *I can't be with you for cocktails tonight, but I hope you'll have one and think of me. I'll be thinking of you. Love, Mark.*

It wasn't much, but it was better than nothing. Around six, I mixed a drink, only remembering after I used the new bottle of St. Germain that I already had an open bottle of it on the bar cart in the living room. Sighing, I stashed the new bottle in the cupboard, figuring it would keep for a while. As I took my first sip of the cocktail, there was a knock on my door.

"Why didn't you answer any of my messages?" Jane demanded.

"Sorry, I turned off my phone."

"You want to tell me what's going on?" Jane held up her phone. The video was playing on her screen. "Did his crazy ex do this?"

"Who else?" I said, standing back to let her in.

"It's high time you called the police." She moved by me slowly. Her pregnancy had turned out to be double the happiness she originally thought. Delighted as she was to be having twins, she wasn't having the easiest time of it. She dropped onto the sofa and fanned herself.

"I doubt that anyone could prove that Donatella sent it," I said. "Do you want something to drink?"

"No, but if you have any Nutella around, bring it out. With a spoon," Jane ordered.

I got it for her, and plopped down on the sofa. "His ex hates my guts. I don't blame her for that. But this harassment needs to stop."

"I seriously think it's time to call the cops. You need a lawyer, too. At this point, you should get a restraining order, but you also have grounds for a civil suit," Jane said.

"A restraining order might stop her if she was stalking me, but Donatella's never shown up in my neighborhood. It's like death by a thousand cuts."

"That box of cockroaches was no small thing," Jane said. "Neither was the tarantula. Look, the law sucks when it comes to protecting women, but it's pretty good with property damage. Since that infestation cost you a lot of money, you have grounds for a lawsuit."

"That would look great," I said, taking a long drink. "The mistress suing the wronged wife."

"She's also trying to ruin your reputation. You can't sit back and do nothing, because it's never going to end. She's the cat and you're the mouse, and she'll bat you around until she finishes you off."

"She wouldn't do that," I murmured. "She'll get over it."

"The evidence is that she won't," Jane said. She kept on talking and talking, but I couldn't hear her clearly. There was a buzzing in my ears and a narrowing of my vision, as if I'd just entered a dark tunnel. Jane's astonished face was the last thing I saw before the black void overtook me.

When I came to, there was a white light above me and a beeping sound beside my head. "What happened?" I asked, my mouth dry as sand.

"You overdosed," said a voice I didn't recognize.

"I… what?"

"You ingested a designer drug known as NBOMe." The doctor was slowly coming into focus as he spoke. "We've been seeing a lot of overdoses from it lately. You could've died."

"But… how?"

"Your friend said you were drinking champagne," the doctor said. "Somebody must've spiked it."

"That's impossible."

"You can't spike an unopened champagne bottle," the doctor said. "But with NBOMe, you need just the tiniest microgram. Someone added it to your drink. I'm going to call the police."

"No, please, don't do that," I begged. "It's all a misunderstanding. I took something a friend gave me. I had no idea it would hit me so hard."

The doctor stared at me long and hard, his mouth twisting cynically. "Your friend must be really into the club scene. That's a hardcore drug."

"Please don't tell the cops," I begged.

He didn't. A while later, they let Jane come in to see me. It was already Sunday afternoon. I'd been knocked out for the better part of a day. "You trying to scare the twins so much that they pop out early?" she demanded. "I thought I was going to have a heart attack."

"I don't know what happened."

"Well, I do. The crazy ex just tried to kill you."

She brought me home, only leaving when I told her that Mark was due in any minute. The first words out of my mouth when I laid eyes on him were, "I drank the cocktail."

"The cocktail?" He gave me a blank once-over. "Are you feeling okay? You look green around the gills."

"I drank the cocktail you sent me."

His expression was bewildered. "I don't know what you're talking about."

"Someone sent me a poisoned drink. I spent last night in the hospital." I found the note on the kitchen counter. I shoved it at Mark. He read it over and dropped it.

"I don't understand," he said. "Someone wrote this, pretending to be me?"

"Someone who knew we'd had a fight that morning," I said. "It's either you, or whoever you told."

"It wasn't me."

"Then who did you tell?"

Mark's left eye started twitching. "No one."

"You told your ex, didn't you?"

"My ex?" He seemed dazed. He was re-reading the note.

"You know she's sent me all kinds of demented little presents," I hissed. "The cockroaches. Broken glass. The tarantula. That dead rat. Now she's trying to kill me."

Mark let out a breath. His whole body seemed to sink down, as if he'd just been deflated. "Oh, Carrie," he said. "Donatella called me on Saturday, some legal business. She asked me why I sounded so awful, and I said..." He swallowed hard. "I mentioned that we'd had an argument. I'm so sorry."

I was furious at Mark, yet relieved on some level. Deep down, my greatest fear was that it was Mark who'd tried to kill me. That fear had taken up residence in the deep recesses on my brain, which was why I'd lied to the doctor and avoided the police. When my brain started to connect the dots, it snagged on the fact that Mark would now inherit the condo if I died. I wondered how Donatella knew about our special cocktail but, for all I knew, it had been their special cocktail, too.

It was terrifying to realize that Donatella wanted me dead, but I knew I had to act. Guilty cowering hadn't gotten me anywhere. That Sunday night, I barely slept. By five-thirty in the morning, I was dressing with greater care than I'd ever exercised before any date. I found my bulletproof interview dress—I thought of it that way, because it had never failed me—and pair of stiletto heels. While Mark was getting out of bed, I was on the subway and headed down to Wall Street.

There was a very long pause at the security desk of Donatella's building when the guard told her that Carrie Barnes was there to see her. But she gave him the go-ahead to allow me upstairs. An assistant greeted me and offered me tea or coffee, and I could only laugh at the idea of drinking anything there. The assistant led me to a corner office with a glorious view of Manhattan's southern flank and the harbor.

"Look what the cat dragged in," Donatella said. She was standing by the window, showing off her glamorous black Prada suit and red skyscraper heels. "This is quite the surprise."

"Is it?"

"Finding my ex-husband's mistress on my doorstep?" She shook her jet-black hair, which fell across one eye and shifted back as if it were under orders. "Has he dumped you already?"

"No. I'm here because of what you've been doing to me."

"You mean laughing at you for taking in my sad wreck of an ex-husband?" She perched on the edge of her desk, looking for all the world like a sleek green-eyed cat.

I stared at her. "What?"

"For the record, I think you're a chump for letting him move in with you. Mark is a vampire. He'll always find fresh victims."

"You've been harassing me. Sending me packages. Horrible things. Bugs and poison and broken glass."

She leaned closer. "I sent you the wreckage of my wedding crystal when I shipped Mark's things over to your apartment," she said. "That only seemed appropriate, given what you were letting yourself in for. But the other things…" She frowned. "Did you say bugs? Cockroaches?"

"Don't play dumb."

"Little Miss Homewrecker, you sent me a box of cockroaches a few weeks before I kicked Mark out."

"That's not true!"

She peered at me closely, as if I were a curiosity that there was some special trick to opening. "Either you sent that box to me, or some other woman Mark is sleeping with did."

"No. You're lying."

"Let me ask you something," she said. "Since Mark moved in, have you seen much more of him than when you were dating?"

"He has a busy schedule."

"Busy with bimbos, yes."

"He visits his mother every weekend."

Donatella laughed. "He's still using that old ruse?" She slid into her chair. "I have seriously misjudged you. I thought you were a nasty, cheap homewrecker who thought she'd triumphed. But you're just a sad little chump."

"How dare you…"

She put up one hand. "I'm sorry, that sounded insulting. What I mean is, I believed you to be a conniving monster. Mark and I had a convenient working relationship."

"Working relationship? What does that mean?"

"It means I got a Green Card and a great deal of freedom when I married him," she said. "My parents were going to disinherit me when they found out I was in love with another woman. So I married Mark and everything worked out. I avoided being disowned and I got to stay with the woman I loved."

"You aren't in love with Mark?"

"I liked him well enough. He could be quite amusing, and he's clever. He fit in perfectly at family parties. Mark, for his part, liked my family's money and having carte blanche, once the family obligations were satisfied."

I could only stare at her.

"If it hadn't been for all of the crazy disruptions, I wouldn't have kicked him out," she said. "But I genuinely started to fear for my safety. I thought you were quite mad."

"This can't be true…"

"Mark's mother died years ago." She typed something on her computer. "My assistant is looking up the obituary. She'll have it in a minute. Look, I don't want to presume anything about your relationship with Mark, but you should know that he's incapable of being honest with women. Even though we had an arrangement, he lied to me for years about visiting his mother on the weekend. That was just a chance for him to play around. He loves the thrill of the illicit." There was a beep and Donatella's head turned to the screen. "There it is. Do you want to read it?"

She swiveled the computer around so I could see the screen. There was an obituary from the *Boston Globe,* dated nine years ago. Mark's mother really was dead. He'd been lying to me as long as I'd known him.

"Be honest," Donatella said. "Did you send any of those awful packages to me? The beef heart with maggots? I couldn't eat for a week after that."

"I swear, it wasn't me."

She studied me carefully. "I believe you," she said. "Clearly that was some other woman Mark is involved with."

When I got home, I went straight to my computer. Could Donatella have faked that obituary? Less than five minutes of searching online revealed that she'd told me the truth. It was Mark who'd been lying to me all along.

I stormed out of the apartment and headed for his office. I didn't even bother to stop at the receptionist's desk. "Hi, Carrie!" she called after me. I made my way to Mark's office, only to find it empty.

"He's out for lunch," said the receptionist, coming down the hall after me. "Are you okay?"

"Not really," I told her.

"If it's an emergency, Alex will know how to reach him," the receptionist said. "This is her office." The door was shut and the receptionist knocked on it. When there was no response, she turned the handle. "She must've stepped out for a minute. Funny, I didn't see her leave. Do you want to wait here for her?"

"Okay. Thanks."

It was a tiny office, albeit one with a door and window. There was nowhere to sit down, so I paced across the four feet of space in front of the desk. The view was mostly of a brick wall of the building next door. But something in the window caught my eye.

It was a tarantula.

My breath caught in my chest. The spider was just a reflection of what was on the screen of Alex's computer. I stepped around her desk. Live animals — find your new best friend! it said at the top of the screen. Underneath were some of the options. The Goliath Bird Eating Tarantula was the one that had caught my eye, but there were others, with names like King Baboon and Cobalt Blue.

I recognized the King Baboon tarantula. That had been in one of the boxes I'd thought Mark's ex-wife sent to me.

Underneath the tarantulas were rows of scorpions.

I backed away from the computer and out of Alex's office, pulling the door shut. I knew I should run away, but I was frozen in place, my hand unable to let the knob go. It couldn't be Alex, I told myself. We were friends. Or friendly, at least. She couldn't be responsible for the barrage of nightmares I'd endured. She wasn't that kind of person.

"Carrie!" Alex's voice shook me out of my thoughts. I half-turned and saw her right beside me. "How are you?"

"Fine," I murmured.

"Better than fine!" There was a huge smile plastered on her face. "Congratulations on your engagement, Carrie! You must be overjoyed."

"Mark told you?"

"Of course." She leaned in conspiratorially. Her blonde curls looked less like a halo and more like pale snakes. "He tells me everything." Her smile never shifted. It remained broad and wide, while her eyes were sharp and fierce.

"Is he here?" I asked.

"No, he's out with an advertiser. Do you want to wait in reception? It's much more comfortable there." She put her hand on my back, steering me away from her office and down the hall. "Let me get you something to drink."

"Thanks, but I should run." I wasn't exaggeration. I scurried into the elevator as fast as my stiletto heels would allow. On the elevator down, I felt like I'd escaped a spider's web. It couldn't be true, I told myself. But things were clicking in my brain, like pieces of a puzzle snapping into place. What a coincidence that the box of cockroaches had only arrived after Mark's possessions had gone into storage. Alex had helped out with that move. She'd been inside my apartment. On my way home, I stopped at the liquor store a couple of blocks from my apartment. The owner knew me and greeted me warmly.

"On Saturday, I got a delivery from you, but I didn't order anything. Do you know who bought it?"

"I don't remember anything being sent to your address. Let me check." He took a look at his computer. "No, nothing."

I found a picture of Alex from the office party and held it up. "By any chance, was this woman in the store?"

He nodded. "Yeah. She bought a half-bottle of champagne. She wanted it bagged like it was being delivered, and a note card, but took it herself."

I trudged home with a dark cloud was hanging over me. How could I have been so stupid? Mark was having an affair with Alex. He had been for some time, obviously. And it was Alex who wanted me dead.

Only it wasn't quite that simple. After I got home, I paced like a caged tiger through the apartment. On a pass through the living room, I noticed that the bottle of St. Germain was missing from the bar cart. It stood out like a missing tooth. I looked for the bottle in the recycling, then went down the hall to the garbage room to search for it in the bin. It was gone.

Mark had made the incriminating evidence disappear.

I'd believed him when he told me he hadn't sent me the poison. Part of me was willing to believe that he hadn't actually tried to kill me. But that twitch by his eye told me he knew who had. Now he was covering up for Alex. His girlfriend had tried to murder me, and he was on her side. Mark might not be up for pulling the trigger himself—he was a lazy coward, after all—but he had no problem encouraging a pack of females to fight over him, even if it was to the death.

When Mark came home, I was ready. "How was your day, darling?" I called.

"Fine." He came into the kitchen, watching me closely. "Alex said you dropped by."

"I did. I thought we might look at rings. But that can wait. I made reservations at Gramercy Tavern. You know, we still haven't celebrated our engagement properly."

"You're right." He gave me he most winning smile. It wasn't really for me; he was delighting in how he'd pulled the wool over my eyes. "We have an awful lot of celebrating to do." I handed him a glass. "Here's to new beginnings."

"To new beginnings." Mark took a big gulp of his drink— he never refused champagne—and grimaced. "Wow, you poured way too much St. Germain into this."

I smiled. "I did. It's from the bottle you sent me on Saturday."

He set the glass down. "This isn't funny, Carrie."

"Did Alex tell you what she did? Is that why you got rid of the bottle?"

"I don't know what you're talking about." He braced himself on the counter with both hands.

"Here's the thing. You got rid of the wrong bottle. The one Alex sent me was in the kitchen cupboard."

His face registered panic. "You wouldn't…"

"All I did was give to you what you what you tried to give me. If there was no poison in that bottle, you're perfectly safe." I held up my phone. "Otherwise, if you want me to call 9-1-1, you have to admit what you did."

He pulled out his phone as he slid to the floor, but it fell out of his quivering fingers and I kicked it out of reach. "Seriously?" he muttered.

I waved my phone in front of him. "The choice is yours."

"Alright!"

"Does that mean guilty as charged?"

He gave me as insouciant a shrug as he could manage from the kitchen floor. "I guess."

"You knew it was Alex all along, didn't you?" I demanded. "What was your masterly plan? Have me sign over the condo and then have her kill me?"

"You make everything sound so dramatic."

I stared at him. "You tried to kill me."

"Alex did."

"With your help. Why?"

He shivered. "It's a great apartment."

I didn't have a comeback for that. If I hadn't frozen in place, I wouldn't dropped to the floor beside him.

"Call 9-1-1," Mark whispered. "You promised."

"I did. But I learned one thing from you."

"What?"

"How to lie."

I waited until he stopped breathing. Then I put on a pair of capacitive gloves, picked up Mark's phone, and carefully pressed his thumb against it to unlock it. Alex, thanks for that bottle of St. Germain, I typed. I don't know why you wouldn't have some with me, but I'm going to do as ordered and mix a cocktail for myself. Carrie's out at dinner with a friend, in case you want to come over.

I pressed send and set the phone on the counter, then wiped my fingerprints off the stem of the glass. I'd already taken care of the bottles, so it was just a matter of pressing Mark's hands on them. Too bad I couldn't add Alex's, but that text would be damning enough. Stepping over Mark's body, I headed for the door. I had a dinner reservation with Jane, and I didn't intend to be late. For the first time in a long while, I was ready to celebrate.

LADYKILLER

"You sure you're up for this?"

Tessa glanced at the cop. "You're going to be outside the door the entire time?"

"I'll be right here. He can't hurt you."

She could feel the weight of his gaze, sizing her up, wondering whether she'd be able to go through with it. She's a big girl, he had to be thinking. Bet she can handle herself. He's not going to be able to do to her what he did to that little redhead.

"Okay." Tessa said. "I'm ready."

The cop opened the door, stepped inside, and gestured for her to follow. Peter sat at a metal table, head in hands. His thinning hair seemed to have gone grey overnight, but maybe that was just the dim light. It wasn't the sort of interrogation cell Tessa had seen on television. There was no mirrored window for the cops to watch through. Instead, there were brown walls, a small window in the door, fluorescent lighting, and an aroma of industrial disinfectant.

Peter was wearing his white monogrammed bathrobe, but it was streaked with rusty stains. That's the redhead's blood, Tessa thought, feeling as if she would vomit. He looked up and got to his feet. "Tessa!"

"Sit down!" barked the cop. "You already murdered one woman tonight, Peter Buckley. You're not getting a chance at a second."

"Kiss my ass," Peter shot back. "My lawyer is going to have me out of here at nine a.m. Then I'm suing your asses for brutality and wrongful arrest."

"Let me talk to him," Tessa said.

"I'm right outside." The cop leaned toward Peter. "Don't try anything, Ladykiller." He retreated and shut the door.

"You bring bail money?" Peter asked.

"But… they haven't set your bail yet."

"The pricks will probably make it five million to set an example. You'll need ten percent of that to get me out of here."

Tessa was stunned by his coolness. There he sat, in a bloody bathrobe, and he was calculating bail. She'd known he was selfish, but this made him seem like a sociopath. "Where am I going to get five hundred thousand dollars?"

"Call my mother."

Peter was a mama's boy, a spoiled rich brat who'd cruised through life on a trust fund and family connections. He'd been handsome once, but that was seventy pounds ago, before his drinking had bloated his features. He was thirty-five, but he looked a decade older.

"She's at her house in Florida right now," Peter added. "But don't tell her exactly what's going on, okay? I don't need her flipping out right now."

"She's going to read about it or see it on TV. She's going to know."

He waved his hand dismissively. "I need her to hear my side of the story first. Then she'll understand."

Tessa let her body sag into a chair. The cold metal against the back of her knees made her shiver. Peter stared at her, his eyes never leaving her face.

"What did you tell the cops about me?" he demanded.

"I said you're my fiancé. I don't know if that's true or not. We've been engaged for two years, but now I find out you're not only sleeping with another woman, you murdered her."

Peter's eyes narrowed, and she realized he was calculating exactly how much truth to tell. "I didn't kill that girl."

"The police said you choked her before you shot her…"

"Bullshit. I didn't lay a hand on her."

"The police were asking me if you like to play… games." Tessa blushed. She'd always gone along with what Peter wanted, but the handcuffs and restraints and whips were entirely his idea.

"Games?"

"They found a bunch of your… toys… in your bedroom." It was hard to get the words out. "They asked if you've ever choked me."

"What did you say?"

"I told them you'd never hurt me in bed," Tessa lied. The bruises on her throat had healed up during her week out of town. Normally she wore turtlenecks or scarves to hide them.

"Good. Don't answer any more of their questions."

"They only let me in here because I answered their questions. They think if you see me, you're going to…"

"Going to what?"

"Confess," Tessa whispered.

"Are you fucking kidding me?" Peter's expression was pure disbelief. "You think I killed that bitch?"

"The police found a naked woman strangled and shot in your house. What else does it look like?"

"This is a set-up. Someone's trying to destroy me." His expression, and his tone, was completely certain.

"Destroy you?"

"There was someone else in my house tonight. He's the one who killed that girl, not me."

"What the hell was that girl doing in your house?"

Peter's eyes narrowed. "I know what you're thinking, but I didn't sleep with her. She's just this girl from my office. Natalia. They brought her in from Brazil a few weeks ago. She's an analyst. Was an analyst."

"Why was she at your house?"

"She had an extensive background in gold mining. I needed analysis of data about a series of mines in South America, and she was the perfect person to do it." It was an explanation that he thought offered enough detail to seem credible.

You lying bastard, Tessa thought, looking down so that her expression wouldn't betray her. An image of Peter and the redhead was seared in her brain. They were tearing off each other's clothing in a hallway with a frantic desire that Peter had never shown for her. Tessa shoved it out of her brain and tried to focus.

"Do you realize how crazy this sounds? It's paranoid. If someone was in the house and killed her, why didn't they kill you, too?"

"Whoever it was wanted to frame me. That's why Natalia is dead." He leaned forward. "You've got to listen to me. Someone else was in the house. When I went upstairs, the light was on in my walk-in closet."

Little hairs rose up on the back of Tessa's neck, but she said, "That's your proof? You probably left it on all day."

"Oh, yeah? Well, what was my mail doing on the kitchen counter?"

Tessa felt her heart skip a beat. "Mail?"

"I noticed it when the cops were going through my house. Mail. On the counter. Someone had brought it inside and put it where I always do."

She opened her mouth, but no sound came out. The mail? Unbelievable.

"I know this sounds crazy," Peter admitted. "But it's the truth."

"What's crazy is why you took a shower while that woman was in the house."

Peter blinked rapidly. "I was really beat, and I had an early morning coming up, so I left her working in the den. I told her to let herself out when she was ready."

"Peter, I've known you for five years. The only time you take a shower before bed is after you have sex. You've got some germ phobia and you go shower for an hour afterwards."

For the first time, his face registered guilt. He'd been caught, and he knew it.

"You're lying to me about not having sex with that woman. You know what, Peter? I'm going to tell that to the police. I'll tell them about every time you tied me up and choked me and pretended you were going to kill me." She stood.

"Tessa, I'm sorry. I swear, it was the first time I ever did anything like this."

His eyes were earnest, but he was still lying. He'd always cheated on her, and she'd been so good at pretending not to notice that he believed she was blind. But now there was a dead girl between them.

"I loved you," said Tessa. "I wanted to marry you. I dreamed about having children with you. And instead you screwed around on me. And now…"

"Listen to me, Tessa. I need you to stand by me. My lawyer says it would look awful if you left. This thing is going to court, and I need you by my side."

As always, it was all about what he wanted. She was supposed to trust him, and he'd do whatever he wanted. But she couldn't do that anymore. Peter was a liar and a cheat. She'd put up with his behavior because, deep down, she thought that he would marry her one day. She wanted to live in his big, beautiful house and call herself Mrs. Buckley. It had all seemed so close, too, since Peter's mother had always liked her. You should marry Tessa, the old woman had told her son. She's a good woman. She'd stand by you, unlike those whores you run around with. Tessa had overheard those very words as she'd listened in on one of their phone calls. But those days of mute fidelity were over.

"I don't want to stay by your side," said Tessa. "You strangled that woman until she was almost dead, and then you shot her in the chest to finish her off, so she couldn't tell anyone what you did."

"If that was true, why didn't I just put her in the freezer in the basement?" Peter grabbed both of her wrists. "Listen to me. I banged her, then went upstairs to shower. I told her she should get dressed and get out. When I came downstairs, she was lying on the floor with blood everywhere and her eyes wide open. I freaked and ran out the door. I thought the killer might still be in my house." He lowered his voice to a whisper. "I was freezing my ass off outside because I was so scared. Don't tell anyone that. They'll think I'm a fucking chicken."

"You were outside when the police came?"

"I was so freaked out, Tessa. I couldn't help it. I ran up and down the street. Then I finally went to Mrs. Chan's door. She's the only person on the block who says hello to me. She called the cops."

"The police think you're pretending to be paranoid," she whispered.

"It was like my real life ended and a horror movie started." Peter's hands tightened on her wrists. "You've got to stand by me.

Call my mother, make her understand I need money, okay? You won't have a problem. She really likes you."

"Okay." Tessa whispered. "Is there anything else you want me to do?"

"Believe in me. Can you do that?"

She nodded and he let go. She got up and left the room without another word.

"You okay?" The cop looked at her with jaded eyes, but there was genuine concern lurking underneath. "I saw him grab your hands, but he kept yapping and I didn't want to break that up."

"It's good you didn't. He would've stopped talking."

"You want to sit down?"

She went downstairs with him and sat on a bench.

"He didn't confess," Tessa said. "He kept saying he didn't kill that girl."

"That's what they all say." The officer snorted. "But he said something else. I can see it in your face."

"He was running around outside, he said. Up and down the block. There's a park just two blocks from his house."

"You think he tossed the gun there?"

"I don't know. There could be another explanation. He thinks… he thinks someone else came into the house and killed her."

"You believe that, I got a bridge to sell you," the cop said. "I'll get uniforms on the park immediately." He stood. "I'll drive you home."

She couldn't answer. Tears slid down her cheeks. In her mind, she was still in Peter's house, walking barefoot down the stairs in a pretty negligee she'd just bought on her trip. She'd heard gasping, animal noises, and she'd watched from the landing as

Peter screwed that redhead, right there on the hallway rug. Before they finished, she'd stepped away, hiding herself in the den, just twenty feet away from them. *I'm beat*, she'd heard Peter announce. *You remember where the bathroom is, right? See you tomorrow, babe.*

The cop handed Tessa a tissue. "They're going to lock him up and throw away the key. You know he deserves that, don't you?"

Tessa wiped her face and blew her nose. Funny how she hadn't cried at Peter's, she thought. After he'd disappeared upstairs, Tessa had stepped out of den. She didn't remember grabbing the power cord from his computer, but it was in her hands, and then against that little redhead's throat. The woman was so stunned she'd barely squeaked. When she dropped to the floor, Tessa had thought she was dead. Feeling as if she were sleepwalking through a nightmare, Tessa marched upstairs, planning to kill Peter. She knew where he kept a gun, knew how to fire it, too. But first she dressed in the spare room where she'd left her clothes. He didn't deserve to see her in the negligee now. She'd reviewed all the ways he'd humiliated her. Death was too good for him, she'd decided. She got the gun from its case in his walk-in closet and went downstairs. She'd planned to put a bullet in a dead woman to seal Peter's link to the death, but there was the redhead, twitching and gasping for breath. Tessa put a hole through her heart. Then she'd pulled up the hood of her coat and went outside, down the block to the park. She'd been careful, wearing gloves when she touched the gun. It wouldn't matter that they'd find her prints all over the massive house. She was there so often. It frustrated her that she'd brought the mail inside when she'd let herself in to surprise Peter. But it would be an inconsequential footnote to the police.

"He wants me to arrange bail for him." Tessa told the officer. "I have to call his mother."

"He won't get bail." The officer patted her arm. "You're such a nice girl. What are you doing with a creep like that?"

MAGPIE

The sheriff who called about my mother-in-law's death sounded genuinely sad about it. "She looked like she was called up to the Lord all peaceful-like," he said, in a deep voice that had a lingering drawl to it. "She went in her sleep, I reckon. I'm sure she didn't feel no pain."

He told me that she'd died of a heart attack, and that it had probably happened a couple of days earlier, given the state in which she was found. "Couple of her near neighbors hadn't seen her about, so they went over, and then they called me. Poor Mrs. Carlow. Let me give you my number so your husband can call me."

I dutifully wrote it down, then folded the paper and put it into my purse. It was just before noon, and Jake was probably with a patient, maybe even in surgery. Telling him the news about his mother over the phone seemed heartless. I could drive to his office and reveal all in person, but given that he hadn't spoken to his mother in years, that seemed like overkill. The news could wait until evening, after he got home. There wasn't anything either of us could do about it now. His mother had lived in the western edge of Ohio, close to the border with West Virginia. Jake and I were in Los Angeles, where we'd moved for his medical practice. We'd been there almost five years, and even though his roots were in hill country and mine were in Cleveland, the West Coast felt completely like home.

Jake surprised me an hour later, the tires of his Porsche squealing into the driveway. I met him at the door.

"My mother's dead," he said. We clung to each other for a while.

"I'm sorry, baby."

"Ludy said they think she died in her sleep."

"Ludy?" I pulled back. "You talked to your sister?"

"She called to tell me what happened."

"She called your office?" My stomach suddenly clenched into knots. "How did she…"

"Never mind that now, Erica. I need to think." He pushed me away and headed for his den, slamming the door behind him. I was too surprised to say anything, or to go after him. He didn't seem sad so much as unsettled. That wasn't a surprise: it was normal to mourn a parent, even one who was a mean, manipulative person. Jake had cut off contact with her years ago because of her abusiveness, and while he was right to do it, I suspected that his conscience wasn't easy right now. Any sense of loss would be made worse if it was accompanied by guilt.

When I knocked on the door, he didn't answer. I listened at it for a moment, but all was quiet. He had alcohol in there, I knew, but no food, so I went to the kitchen and made him a sandwich. I put it on a tray and wrote a little note on an index card—I love you, baby—and left it in front of the door, knocking to let him know it was there. An hour later, it was untouched, like a rejected peace offering at the altar of an angry god.

That was when I started to worry. My husband was a man with a tender heart; he found it hard to hold a grudge against anyone, no matter how deserving. It had been so painful for him to cut off contact with his mother, even though he'd done so for reasons any sane person would understand. You couldn't put up with a toxic person just because you were related to her; you still had to draw a line somewhere. Mrs. Carlow had actually made it easier for Jake by ignoring him. Jake had sent her a birthday card once, after they cut off contact. I only knew about it because his mother had crossed out her name with a spidery X and wrote RETURN TO SENDER on the envelope, so the card boomeranged back to our house. How did you mourn a mother like that?

I wandered aimlessly through our house, wondering what to do. Jake needed help, but I wasn't sure how to give it to him. We'd been together for a dozen years, and yet sometimes I found it hard to understand him.

When I knocked again on the door of his study, he ignored me. But he hadn't locked me out, and the knob turned under my hand. I stepped over the tray and went inside. The blinds were drawn, but I could see Jake's silhouette at his desk. He seemed to be staring into space. I didn't hear the music at first, it was turned so low. The lyrics came as a whisper: "Oh, Death, oh death, please spare me over till another year."

"What is it, Erica?" Jake's voice was just as quiet as the singer's.

I'd prepared a speech in my mind, but it slipped away. "I'm sorry," I blurted out. "I wish I knew what to do to help you, baby."

Jake just looked at me with that hard, flat expression that came over him when he got lost inside his own thoughts. Normally, I could cajole him out of it, but I had a feeling that I wouldn't be able to this time. He was too bitter and raw right now. He was dangerous at the moment, liable to do something rash if I didn't pay very close attention to him. "There's nothing anyone can do now. What's done is done."

"It's normal to have conflicted feelings in a situation like this. It's..."

"Erica, please cut out the bullshit psychobabble. I can't listen to it now."

That made a lump swell in my throat. Jake almost never cursed, certainly not at me. He was more depressed than I'd realized.

"I have to go out there," he muttered.

"You what?"

"I need to go home for my mother's funeral."

"Jake, she's gone and nothing is going to change that. Going to her funeral isn't going to help her. It's just going to drag you back to a place you hate and bring back painful memories."

"I'd rather have the painful memories than whitewash the past."

"You're so busy at work," I pointed out. "They need you at the clinic. You can't just leave them in the lurch."

"Why? Because some starlet wouldn't get her boob job? Or maybe some spoiled teenager wouldn't get her bumpy nose fixed?"

"You're picking ridiculous examples. You know you do wonderful work. Important work. Think of all the little kids you've helped." Jake occasionally spent his weekends performing surgery, for free, on poor kids from the inner city whose parents could never have afforded to fix their cleft palates and other disfigurements.

He rubbed his temples. "It's not enough."

"Look, let's make a donation in your mother's honor. I was looking online, and there's this one association that focuses on heart attack and stroke prevention for women."

Jake stared at me for what felt like a very long time. "How did you know my mother died of a heart attack?"

"Oh, I..." I felt terrible for not telling him about the sheriff's call sooner. But when he'd come home, he'd already known that his mother was dead, and he'd disappeared into his den before I'd had the chance to say anything. "The sheriff who found her called here, right before you came in. I was going to call you, but then I was thinking I should tell you in person, and then you came home and you already knew…"

He put his hand up. "I don't want to hear it. Just leave me alone."

I swallowed hard and backed out of the room. "Let me know if you need anything," I said, pulling the door behind me. Just before it closed, I stopped and poked my head back in the room. "I love you, baby."

Jake just stared at me. I shut the door and tried not to panic.

Jake surprised me late that night, leaving his den and joining me in bed. He didn't want comfort or sleep. He wanted me. Maybe that was the only way he could forget his pain. By the time he was done, our sheets were sticky with lust and sweat, and I fell asleep in his arms, feeling at peace with the world.

In the morning, I woke up alone. Jake's gym bag was gone, and I thought he'd gone to the club early to play squash. I was glad, because I thought that was a sign Jake had turned a corner, that the crisis I'd felt was impending was going to be averted.

But then I realized Jake's laptop was gone. Sitting in its place on his desk was a white sheet from a company that made some sort of line-filling injectible gel. I had to go home, it read.

I crumpled it into a ball and threw it against the wall. Home? He still thought of that hellhole in the sticks as home? That turned my stomach. What about our home together? What about our life together? I picked up the phone, looked at the numbers

Jake had called recently, and hit redial. What did he think he was doing? Was he determined to ruin his life? Jake could be impulsive, acting first and worrying about consequences later. I had to save him from himself.

In theory, I knew where I was going. I got on a red-eye flight that night that took me from Los Angeles to Charlotte, and then a connecting flight on a commuter plane to Charleston, West Virginia. It was easy enough to rent a car and follow the highway west, to where it ran alongside the Ohio River, but once I crossed the bridge, I was on my own. Google Maps could only take me so far through the barren, miserable wilderness of hill country.

Jake had taken me to visit his family there only once, just before we got married. We'd been engaged forever, and he was close to finishing his medical residency. "I can't marry a girl my family hasn't met," he told me. That settled it.

"They're not going to like me," I warned him. "They're going to see me as some city snob in high heels."

"They'll love you," Jake soothed me. "They already know how smart and hard-working you are. That you were a scholarship student like I was. They know you were raised by your mom, and that she died when you were in high school…"

"You told them that?"

"It's nothing to be ashamed of, Erica. You should be proud that you started with nothing and worked hard to get where you are."

"What else did you tell them about me?" I seethed.

"Everything that's wonderful about you," he said, kissing me. "And I want you to see how wonderful it is there. You're going to love it."

I knew he was wrong about that, but I didn't have the heart to tell him. I'd worked hard to break free from government housing and food stamps, and I hadn't done that so I could live in a mountain shack. I had other plans.

The visit went just as badly as I knew it would. "Didn't think I'd be seeing you 'round here. Ain't you able to come up with some excuse not to darken my doorstep?" Those were the first words out of Mrs. Carlow's mouth when she saw us at the door. Jake, being his usual sweet self, mollified her. But she fixed her narrow blue eyes on me and pursed her lips, looking me up and down. Sometimes, when people met me, they told me I looked exotic and used that as cover to ask about my race. Mrs. Carlow didn't ask that, but I felt those cold eyes parsing pieces out, not liking any of them. While Jake was able to thaw her out, she remained cold and rude with me. She didn't come out and say anything directly. Her insults were carefully couched in statements that were hard to answer.

"Them's some fine clothes you have," she'd told me. "What's that old saw? Fine feathers make fine birds?" She turned to Jake. "Cousin Hark's wife just walked out on him. She was one who always thought real well of herself." Her expression made it clear what she thought of women who thought well of themselves.

I knew, even then, that Mrs. Carlow thought she could chase me off. What she hadn't realized was that I'd already made up my mind about Jake and my own future, and that there wasn't a damn thing she could do about it. What she couldn't have realized was how much I wanted her to hate me.

I was thinking of that visit as I steered my rental car along the roads. Nature was something I loved in healthy doses. Being surrounded by hills and fields with no indications of people nearby — except for occasional tractor-crossing signs made me nervous. When it got to be too much for me, I stopped the car and turned on my cell phone. Jake had tried to call me several times before I'd boarded my flight; I hadn't answered, and once I'd turned off my phone I hadn't turned it back on. He had to be sweating by now, wondering why I wasn't answering. I dialed his number and he answered immediately. "Why haven't you been answering your phone? I've been worried sick about you."

"Why did you go running off in the middle of the night? Why didn't you tell me?"

He sighed. "I knew if I did, I'd never get here. I just had to do it then, Erica. It was important. Don't be upset, okay?"

"Oh, I'm upset all right. Especially because I'm sitting in the middle of nowhere trying to figure out how to get to where you are."

It took him a second to absorb that. "You flew out here? To be with me?"

"You didn't think I was just going to wait at home for you, did you, baby?"

"I was worried you'd be so angry you might file for divorce," he admitted in a sheepish tone.

"I'd never do that to you, baby," I said, and I meant it.

The only person who seemed distinctly unhappy to see me was Kady. When Jake brought me back to her house, where all of the family was meeting, her mouth pursed, just like her mother's had when she'd met me. Kady had been friendly enough when I'd encountered her before, but now I saw bitterness and recrimination in her eyes. But that might only have heated up after her husband, a ruggedly handsome man named Ry, hugged me for longer than was strictly necessary.

"I'm sorry about your mother," I told her. She nodded, keeping her eyes on my face. Her own was red and blotchy, and her eyes were swollen. Her two young sons stopped running around long enough to inspect me, then took off, laughing. In the living room, a collection of cousins sat around drinking and laughing. It didn't seem as if anyone missed Mrs. Carlow much.

"You got here in a hurry," Kady said to me.

"It's a tough time for Jake. I wasn't going to leave him alone."

"You sure that's the reason? Or were you afraid he'd come back here and go native?" Kady's voice was more refined and less country than her mother's had been, but it had the same twangy undertones.

"Go native?"

"You know exactly what I mean. You're the reason he never came home. Jake was going to come back and be a doctor here. You wouldn't let him do that."

"That's ridiculous. Jake never wanted to come back here."

"Yes, he did, and you're the one who ruined it. You're the one who got him to throw his life away, doing them plastic surgeries instead of proper medicine." As her temper heated up, her diction slipped.

"Last time I checked, Jake was an adult who could make his own decisions."

"You're a thief, nothing more."

"Really?" I rolled my eyes. "That was what your mother said, too. That was why Jake stopped speaking to her, you know."

"Oh, I know that full well. You got a hell of a nerve coming back here. You stole Mama's earrings just like she said you did. You're a thief and a liar."

"I didn't steal anything," I said, my voice calm. I had the truth on my side. Maybe I had told Jake a lie or two for his own good, but I'd never stolen anything.

"Mama caught you in her room that time Jake brought you to her house!"

"I just wanted to see the photographs. There was nothing wrong with that."

"Then she found her pearl earrings were gone. You took them. It had to be you."

"She went and grabbed my purse and dumped it out on the table because she thought they were in there," I said. "Then, when she found they weren't, she practically ripped off my blouse because she thought I was hiding them in my bra. She was wrong."

"You had them," Kady insisted. "You know what Mama called you? Magpie, on account of you seeing something good and shiny and not being able to keep yourself from thieving."

The insult rankled, but I wasn't going to let that show. "Your mother was delusional. Maybe that runs in the family."

"I don't know how you got them earrings outta the house, but you did. You stole them, sure as you stole my brother away from his home. But you're in for a surprise, because this time Jake's gonna stay where he belongs."

"You go on thinking that if it makes you happy," I said. "But after the funeral, we're going home."

❖

Jake and I went to his mother's house the next day. It was only my second time there, but I remembered it well. It was old-lady fussy, with plastic over the sofa and white doilies on the tables. There were little carvings and statuettes on every available surface, including a series of owls that were downright spooky.

"I'm surprised you were willing to come along for this, but I'm glad you did, Erica."

"I couldn't let you go through your mother's things by yourself, baby. That would be too stressful."

"Kady's already done a lot of the work. I'm just looking for anything I want to keep. Kady's already got the photo albums and Mama's jewelry and the family Bible at her place."

"Wow. She lost no time helping herself to your mother's things."

"Don't start, Erica. Please. This is stressful enough."

I bit my tongue. The last thing I needed to do was fight with Jake right now. I noticed his verbal lapse—Mama—and that made me nervous. Old habits came back quickly, didn't they? But I was also slightly annoyed with myself. Of course Kady took her mother's jewelry. If I'd planned ahead, I would have gotten a pair of earrings like Mrs. Carlow had owned—baroque pearls on 14-karat gold stems—and set them in her jewelry box, then remarked on them while Jake was nearby. It was too late for that now. Better to stick with my original plan.

While Jake was going through the record collection, I slipped out of my dress. For a moment I debated leaving my bra and panties on and letting Jake remove them, but then I pulled them off, too. It was important not to have any margin for error. I went up behind him and wrapped my arms around his waist from behind.

"This isn't a good time, Erica. I can't right now."

"Oh, baby, you always can."

We went back and forth like that for a while. I thought he might give in, but all of those owls watching had a negative effect on his libido. After a while I sighed and said I was going to the bathroom.

"You'll keep an eye on my purse and stuff, right?" I called from the doorway.

Jake turned. It was important the he know I was completely naked. "Sure. But no one's running off with it."

I went to the bathroom and closed the door. Everything in the room was pink or had a floral print on it. There was even a pink owl sitting on the vanity. It made me feel a little self-conscious as I knelt down and opened the vanity. Inside were half-used bottles of shampoo, boxes of baking soda, and other junk I didn't care about. Instead, I ran my fingers along the inside ledge just above the doors. When I hit something that felt like hardened putty, I pried it loose. There, encased in hardened gum, were the missing earrings, just as I'd left them. When I pried them free, I noticed that the pearls were looking a little gray. Of course, pearls needed contact with skin to keep their luster. These had been neglected for five years.

"You won't believe what I found," I told Jake when I came out. I put the earrings into his hand.

"Where did you get these?"

"They were in the bathroom."

"They've been in the house all this time?" He frowned. "Where were they, exactly?"

"In the medicine cabinet."

"Why were you in the medicine cabinet?"

"Why does that matter? I was looking for a bandaid, okay?" This wasn't the reaction I'd expected at all. "The point is, your mother accused me of stealing her earrings, and they've been here all this time."

"I don't think these are the same ones. They look fake."

"If they're fake, it's because they were always fake!" I was exasperated. "Those are the earrings."

"How can you be sure?"

I stopped, realizing that that was a trick question. That time we'd visited, I'd denied even seeing the earrings. How could I claim I knew what they looked like. "I guess I just got excited when I saw them. Like maybe your mother realized she was wrong." I started to get dressed. I'd wanted Jake to know that I hadn't carried anything into the bathroom with me, but now that seemed pointless.

"I'll give them to Kady. She'll know them better than me."

But Kady wasn't any more convinced than her brother when she saw them. "These look like cheap-ass imitations. Not the real thing," she said.

They did look like fakes, truth be told. But that wasn't my fault.

"You think they're Mama's?" Jake asked.

"I'd bet they're replacements put there by someone with a guilty conscience." Kady looked at me. I fought the urge to kick her and turned to the window. Her husband, Ry, was outside, playing with their boys. This trip wasn't going as I expected it to at all. I needed to do something to fix that fast, before it was too late.

Hilary Davidson

"We need to talk," Jake told me on the morning of his mother's funeral.

"What is it, baby?"

"We've been out in Los Angeles for five years. I'm not happy there. I don't like the work I'm doing. I trained as an otolaryngologist, and what am I doing? I'm making starlets look like Barbie."

"But you're doing so well. They love you at the clinic. And every month you volunteer…"

"It's not enough, Erica. I want to help people here. That was always my plan. I just got sidetracked."

"Sidetracked?" I stared at him. "You have a great life. These people here, don't you think any of them would kill to get what you have? You got out. That's what the people here want to do."

"It's not like your old neighborhood, Erica. There are a lot of people happy to be living out here. I'm sick of being in the city."

"This is just guilt talking," I said. "Your mother died, and now you feel bad. Never mind that she was an evil person who told lies about people to try to manipulate you."

"Erica." He looked at me, his face serious. "That time we visited her… you didn't accidentally take her earrings or anything like that, did you?"

"I can't believe you're even asking." Now I was getting angry. "I told you then, and I can't believe you're making me say it again, but I swear to you, I didn't steal her earrings, accidentally or otherwise."

"It's just… it's kind of funny you found those replacements. It is a little weird."

"I guess your whole family thinks I'm a thief and a liar."

"Of course not, Erica. I'm sorry, I just…"

I walked out of the room. We were silent on the drive to the church; at least, I was. Jake made a few attempts at conversation, which I ignored. At the church, I sat next to him, but stared straight ahead, ignoring him. Jake was busy consoling Kady, who wore a frumpy black dress and a big black hat with a veil. The two of them stood over their mother's casket for the longest time.

"Can't say I miss the old bat," Kady's husband, Ry, whispered to me. "She was a pain in the ass. She was always fighting with somebody."

I'd thought to pack a form-fitting black designer dress that hugged my curves. Jake was too preoccupied to notice, but it didn't escape Ry.

Back at the house for the wake, Ry whispered, "So, Kady says you planted fake pearls at her mama's house. She's all steamed about it."

"What makes you think I did something?" I smiled at him.

He grinned back. "You're the kinda gal who's always up to something, Erica."

"Well, it's never good to be boring." We clinked glasses. Ry was drinking bourbon, while I was guzzling more wine than I'd planned. It was frustrating, knowing I was right about something and not being able to prove it.

"It must've been awful, living only an hour away from Mrs. Carlow," I said.

"Lemme tell you about that." He did, and he made me laugh, which earned some dark looks from Kady. Then Ry followed me when I went upstairs.

"Don't think I didn't notice you staring at me," I said. We were standing in the guest bedroom where Jake and I were staying. I looked in the mirror and unpinned my hair.

"Don't think I didn't notice you enjoying it," he answered.

"Do you think anyone will come up here?"

"Not if we're quiet."

I pounced on him. Ry was a surprisingly good kisser. I thought about Kady's sour face and figured he must be getting practice somewhere else. He started to unzip my dress. "No," I whispered. "Rip it off."

"But it must've cost a pretty penny."

"Rip it off," I ordered. There was a sound like a series of pops as the fabric broke apart at the seam.

"Oh, I like this," Ry said.

"I bet you do." With that, I reached out and raked my nails over his face.

"What the fuck?" He pushed me away and touched his skin. I let out a bloodcurdling scream, opened the door, and ran from the room. Jake was on the stairs and I ran into his arms. Then I sobbed and sobbed.

The trip home to Los Angeles was uneventful. Jake was silent most of the time. I wore a little eye mask so that I could sleep, but occasionally I would tug at the corner to watch him. He was drinking whiskey, his jaw taut. Every so often his eyes would narrow, but mostly he just drank.

"Do you think I did the right thing?" I asked him. "By not pressing charges against Ry, I mean."

"I think that would've been a mistake," Jake answered. "Those kids don't need their dad locked up in jail."

"At long as he doesn't attack some other woman..." I mused.

"He won't do that," Jake muttered.

That made me frown, but he didn't say anything else and I let the matter drop. I fell asleep somewhere over the Midwest, and when I did, I dreamt I was back in Mrs. Carlow's house.

"What are you doing in here?" she snapped at me, just as she had in real life. I was in her bedroom, standing in front of her dresser. There were framed photos there, of her dead husband and her children, and one of Mrs. Carlow herself before she was Mrs. anything.

"Nothing," I said, brushing past her and walking down the hall, turning into the bathroom. My heart was racing as I locked the door. I opened my hand and saw the earrings in my palm. There was a beautiful black bird sitting in the open window, and I dropped the pearls into her mouth. Then magpie flew away until she was just a distant dot on the horizon, getting as far from that place as fast as she could.

GOOD BONES

Even before Tom found the baby's bones, he'd seen omens that the old house was a death trap. There was that little fire in the kitchen that revealed ancient knob-and-tube wiring. Next, a pipe burst in the second-story bathroom, warping the floor and damaging the kitchen ceiling. Which element will strike next? Tom joked to his wife. Earth, it turned out: one spring morning they found a dead cat in their backyard, its tail protruding from under the rickety wooden stoop, which turned out to be infested with termites.

Tom wanted to sue the previous owners, who must have bribed the house inspector to give the place a pass. We can get out of this, he told his wife. But Monica hadn't wanted out. She was the one who'd been seduced by the Victorian house in the first place. Tom had watched her fall in love as the real estate agent first walked them through. Monica was entranced by the faded glamour whispered by the high ceilings and decorative moldings and lead-glass windows. It has good bones, she said, as if that answered everything. For a time, it had, while they were still living in the condo and the house was their weekend project. Tom almost got used to the knot of nerves that tightened in his stomach as they uncovered more defects in it. But finding the bones inside the wall was too much.

All Tom had wanted was to hang a picture in the first-floor hallway. It was Monica's idea, of course. Her to-do list was filled with tasks Tom considered unnecessary luxuries: fill vases with orchids, cover walls with oil paintings, load rooms with antiques. She talked about setting up a photo shoot for *House & Home* magazine. Tom wanted a working shower. But since Monica considered the claw-foot porcelain bathtub romantic, it was staying put — and Tom was standing, at ten o'clock on a Friday night, in the hallway with a hammer in one hand and a nail in the other. "Here?" he asked.

"A bit lower. I said a bit." Monica wasn't trying to hide her exasperation. Tom slid the nail up a hair's breadth and got another sigh. "That'll do," Monica mumbled through a mouthful of shiraz.

For a split second, Tom pictured his boss's head on the wall, shriveled to the size of the nail. That was a mistake, he realized, as he brought the hammer down. He'd used too much force. Instead of the nail sinking into the plaster, the wall crumbled beneath it.

"I can't believe you did that!" Monica screeched. "You moron!"

Something in Tom snapped. He hated the house, wished he'd never set eyes on it. Dropping the hammer, he kicked the wall, coughing hard as plaster dust filled the air. There was a yawning hole now, big enough for a dwarf to step through. Maybe it was a black hole that would suck them all in, Tom thought. That was what the house was: a gaping void that made money vanish.

Monica gasped and clutched her glass to her chest. She was staring into the hole, her lips, purplish from the wine, hanging apart. Tom followed her gaze and saw gleaming white just inside.

"That's a hand," Monica whispered.

Tom crouched to touch it. It was delicate, like the skeleton of a tiny monkey he'd seen at the museum when he was a kid. The index finger pointed accusingly while the other digits were curled into a fist. Everything else was hidden inside crumpled newspaper. Tom reached for the bundle and set it on the floor, drawing back the powdery pages. Inside was a blanket that might once have been white. The little skeleton wore a powder-blue pair of sleepers with snaps up one side. There was no sign of flesh or blood and no smell other than the dank mold of the rambling old house.

Monica knelt opposite Tom. "A baby," she said. They stared at it for a moment. "We have to call the police."

"Look at the date on the paper." Tom pointed to the top of the page, close to a photograph of Joseph Stalin. *July 19, 1945.*

"This fucking house is cursed." Monica stood and finished her wine. "What a nightmare."

"We can call the police tomorrow."

"Tomorrow's Saturday. In case you've forgotten, I'm working this weekend." Monica turned and headed for the kitchen. Tom watched her silhouette pouring more wine. Since she'd lost her job as a magazine editor, she was angry all the time. Tom worked weekends, too, but at least he hadn't been laid off. Not yet, anyway. He'd worked at the same TV station for a decade, but over the past six months, he felt like he'd just started there. He couldn't even get his reports on the air. His new boss, Richard, treated him like an errand boy. They'd competed for years as reporters, and Richard had always been a snotty bastard. Now that he was a big-shot producer, he sent Tom after stories that were fool's errands, then forced him to edit other reporters' tapes.

"Sorry, honey," said Tom. "I forgot. At least you're going to a spa."

"I have to write about that fucking spa, you know. It's not like I'm going there for fun. If you had any balls at all, you'd get me into TV." She'd been freelancing since she'd been laid off, working long hours for virtually no money. Tom's income supported them, just barely. They didn't have money for dinners out anymore, or health-club memberships, or vacations. Any discretionary income went straight into that money-pit of a house.

"I'm sure it'll be a great story," Tom said brightly. "Who's it for again?"

"Why? Are you going to start pitching women's magazines? Maybe you should. Maybe that's your real vocation."

She was always so hostile, acting like everything was his fault. Moving into this house was supposed to be a dream come true for them. Sure, it was in The Junction, a Toronto neighborhood named for its proximity to multiple train tracks. But the area was better than it used to be, and the bones of the house hinted at its potential: big windows, a sweeping staircase, enough bedrooms for the kids they'd talked about having.

"I'm taking the train at one," Monica added. "Get it out of my sight in the meantime."

"Where should I put it?"

"I don't care. Maybe the basement." The basement was the nastiest part of the house, with a dirt floor that a previous owner had dug up but never filled in. Tom and Monica didn't even use it for storage.

"Yikes. What if there are more down there?" Tom said.

"More what?"

"Skeletons."

"You are disgusting," Monica said. "Sometimes it makes me sick just to listen to you."

Tom spent Saturday trailing after a reality-show contestant who'd blown out his vocal cords on TV. But that had happened a year ago and no one would remember the guy's name now, except Richard, who seemed to be scraping some particularly foul assignment barrel. Tom knew the segment would never air, and felt guilty for putting the rasping ex-singer through it. That evening, he cracked open a beer and called Ramsay, a cop he'd met when he was a student reporter on the crime beat. Ramsay was retired now, and complained about having too much time on his hands.

"What, the wife abandoned you again?" Ramsay asked in his gravelly voice when Tom swung open the front door. He squinted at the terrible squeal. "Where's she at this time?"

"At a spa. It's for some magazine."

"Thought I was doing well when Maureen passed on," Ramsay said. "Three years now, God rest her wicked soul. Thought I'd like the peace and quiet. But it makes you daft after a bit, being alone, you know?"

"Monica's been going away as much as she can since we had to move into the house. Can't say I blame her."

"Ingrate. Look at that fancy molding," said Ramsay. "Real craftsmanship, putting the like of that in. Don't see that kind of work anymore."

"I'll sell it to you. Please. Take it off my hands."

"Too bad the market sank like a stone. Otherwise you could've flipped it, made some serious coin." Ramsay's pale blue eyes zeroed in on the massive hole in the hallway wall. "Your handiwork?"

"Yep." Tom led him back to the kitchen and opened another beer. "I didn't think it could go any further downhill. But things keep breaking."

Ramsay stared at the sagging, waterlogged ceiling. "It's falling down around your ears, lad."

"Monica wanted this house."

"Sure, once it's fixed up. Then it'll be a showpiece. When you're ninety." Ramsay took a long drink. "How'd you end up moving in so fast? I thought the plan was to do the work first."

Tom shrugged. What could he say? When the real-estate market had started to tank, they'd gotten a great offer for his condo, which Tom had bought long before he'd met Monica. Take the deal! his agent had screamed. The market is going into the toilet! That agent had been right, and they'd been lucky to sell the condo when they had. But they'd moved into a house that was essentially uninhabitable.

"I could help you get this pile straightened out," Ramsay offered. "I miss doing all that tinkering since my house was sold. I'm a dab hand with all that. I know plenty of boys in construction. I love working in the garden. Such a green yard we had."

"Thanks, Ramsay. I'll get around to it one day."

"No rush. It's only June, mind."

Then he took Ramsay to the basement, opening the door from the kitchen and padding down the cold metal steps. Something midway between damp and rotten made him wince. A 60-watt bulb dangled from a wire, casting low shadows and making the dug-up dirt floor look like a bottomless pit. The bundle of bones and broadsheets was on the bottom step, where he'd left it.

"Poor wee thing." Ramsay lifted it as gently as he would have a live infant. "A sin, whoever did the like of this."

"The couple who sold us the house had it for thirty years. Going by the date on the paper," Tom pointed to July 19, 1945, "this goes back way before them."

"I was born in '42," Ramsay said. "Back then, if a girl got knocked up, she went away to a home."

"I was wondering about that. If a girl gave birth in the house, and the baby was stillborn or died just after, why not bury it properly?"

"Maybe it wasn't a girl. Maybe it was a woman with a husband over in Europe. The war was ending then. It was over in Europe, almost over in Asia."

"But to give birth and…"

"It doesn't make logical sense," said Ramsay. "Most crimes don't. But I'll tell you one thing. Whoever put this child in the wall was hiding more than a dead body."

When Monica came home Sunday night, she asked Tom if the bones were gone. Good. I don't want to even think about it again, she said, disappearing upstairs and taking a bottle of shiraz into the bath with her. But on Monday, she called him at work, clearly agitated. "What did you do with the dead baby?"

"Ramsay took it," Tom said.

"You just let him take the bones?"

"He's bringing them in to the lab. It's not a big priority for the police, but they're going to investigate and later they'll bury…"

"Did it ever occur to you that finding the bones was a great story? No wonder you're such a failure as a reporter. You don't even know when you have a good story under your nose."

She hung up. Tom stared at the receiver. Was Monica having lunch with one of her editors, and mentioned their sad discovery? He glanced towards his boss's office, but the door was closed and the light was off. Tom was relieved. He didn't want to see that superior smirk on Richard's face, the one that said I know you're clinging by your fingernails, errand boy.

Tom called Ramsay, who gave him the name of the investigating officer. "But don't be expecting DNA results," Ramsay cautioned. "They're backed up over there with rape kits. The poor wee thing has waited this long. He'll just have to wait a little longer."

When Richard returned to the office, he called Tom in for a meeting. As Richard sat back, long legs stretched out, Tom went over his developing stories. Richard tossed a baseball in the air and kept his eyes on it. He was barely listening.

"I'm calling this piece Toxic City," said Tom, describing a series of health reports that showed that Toronto was becoming increasingly polluted.

Richard laughed and shook his head. "Why're you coming to me with this stuff, Tommy?" he said. "You trying to bore the pants off me?"

Tom was five foot nine, three inches shorter than Richard, and he hated it when Richard called him Tommy. "It's an important story. One we should be covering."

"Such an earnest boy." Richard smirked. "Got anything else?"

Tom thought about what Monica had said about the dead child. "Human-interest piece about a couple who renovate a house and find a baby's skeleton inside the walls."

Richard looked at him directly for the first time since Tom had walked in. "Is the couple telegenic?"

"Monica and I found the bones in our house."

"Whoa." Richard tossed the baseball in the air a few times. "Okay," he said finally. "Run with that. And gimme your research on the Toxic City thing."

It was only at the end of the day that Tom heard, from another reporter at the station, that they were doing the Toxic City story. It had just been assigned to her.

Tom had no time to research his story that week. On Tuesday, Richard sent him to cover the story of a hiker who'd been found in Algonquin Park. The man had disappeared in March, and his defrosted body had just been discovered. There was no reason to be up there for days, but Richard insisted. "Don't come back till you got something unique. Gimme an angle." By the time Tom came home Friday, he was glad to collapse into his own bed, even if he was worried about the floor under it. Early Saturday morning, his cell phone woke him up.

"Having a bit of a lie-in on the weekend, are we?" Ramsay chuckled. "'Course, you've got a pretty wife, so there's incentive."

Tom stretched out. Monica's side of the bed was cold. She'd left on Friday to visit her mother in Montreal, and he was alone again. "She's away right now. What's up?"

"Fuck me, she's off again? Pardon my French. How can she do that?"

Tom was annoyed, but he wasn't going into it with Ramsay. Monica had said her mother wasn't feeling well. As a peace offering, she'd left a big bouquet of red roses in their bedroom. Tom didn't care much for flowers, but he appreciated the thought. "Forget it, Ramsay. Tell me what's new."

"Got the autopsy report on that baby. It was murder."

Tom sat up, his heart racing. "How can they tell? You said they wouldn't know anything for a while…"

"I forgot what sick bastards they are at the lab," Ramsay said. "Give 'em a mystery that's older than they are and they're pissing themselves to get at it. They found a cranial fracture. Poor wee thing was only a few weeks old."

"Who would do that?"

"That's where we hit a dead end. A fire gutted the house in '44. The owners moved west, to Vancouver. The house was uninhabited till April '47."

"I'm on it," Tom said.

It had been a long time since Tom had worked on a story he cared about. He interviewed his neighbors and tracked down those who'd moved away. He found people who'd known the different owners of the house. He reviewed the ownership records in a musty municipal office. He turned up nothing.

Monica quickly lost interest. "Seriously, all you can talk about is a dead baby," she pointed out one night. "You need a life."

"You should come back from Montreal," Tom said. "Obviously I'm going crazy alone in this house."

There was a long pause.

"I could come visit on the weekend," Tom added.

"My mom is having problems. It wouldn't be a good time for you to come out. Anyway, you've got your dead baby story to work on."

Monica made light of it, but Tom was serious. There was a raw sense of justice in him that was repulsed by the murder. It made it hard to think about anything else.

Tom knocked on the door of a small house in Toronto's Cabbagetown. It was a simple worker's cottage, built when Irish laborers dominated the neighborhood, yet it had elegant lines and big windows. The front garden teemed with ferns and Bleeding Hearts and Queen Anne's Lace.

"Hello," said the woman who answered the door. She was seventy, judging by the lines in her face, and there was something disarmingly sweet about her smile. She wore a pink dress with a pattern of white flowers, and she twirled a pink necklace of beads at her throat. "How are you?"

"Fine, thanks," said Tom, surprised by her warmth. "I'm looking for…"

"Marie, did you answer the door?" demanded another woman. As she came closer, moving cautiously, Tom saw that she was a decade older than Marie, with an expression twisted by anger or pain, or some combination of the two. She wore a plain navy dress, sensible navy shoes and a gold cross. "What do you want?" she barked.

"My name is Tom Lee. I work for a television show called…"

"I don't watch television and I don't like people who do." the woman announced.

"I was hoping to talk to someone who knew Donald O'Neill."

"What for?" snapped the woman.

"He was our father," said Marie, smiling shyly.

"Go back to your room. I'll handle this."

"But he was our father, Suzy!" Marie looked stricken.

"Donald O'Neill ran a construction business," Tom said. "O'Neill and Sons. He did construction work in 1945 on a house on Clendenan Avenue in The Junction."

Suzy's mouth froze in a grim line. "Get away from my door, do you hear me? If you come back, I'll call the police." She pulled her sister back and slammed the door in Tom's face.

"Found any new skeletons in your closet?" Richard asked him the next morning. He was looking very pleased with himself these days, and Tom wished he knew why. It was as if he had uncovered a secret and was letting it melt in his mouth like a chocolate. "I think you're spending too much time with dead people, Tommy."

"I've got leads," Tom mumbled. He was on hold with a structural engineers' association, and he cradled the phone between his ear and shoulder.

"Well, I've waited long enough for something to pan out," Richard announced. "I've gotta piece about spas that cater to couples that needs to be filmed. You're on it, Tommy."

"You've got to be kidding. I don't do spas."

"Really? Too good for that, huh?" Richard pressed a button on Tom's phone, ending the call. He slapped a blue Post-It note on Tom's monitor. HealthWinds. Tom knew nothing about spas, yet the name seemed familiar. "Be there at two today, or you're out on your ass."

At two that afternoon, Tom was still sitting in front of the little house in Cabbagetown. It was how he wished his own house looked, he realized. Tidy and clean and inviting.

The O'Neill sisters weren't at home. Tom had rung the bell several then, then let himself through the little gate at the side of the house and peered through the windows.

"Can I help you?" called a neighbor out an open window. The man had a cordless phone in his hand, probably had already dialed 911.

"Process server," said Tom. He'd spent enough time climbing around places he wasn't supposed to be, and he was a good liar. "Looking for Suzy O'Neill."

"Oh." The neighbor put the phone down and wandered away. Tom went back to the front of the house, leaning against the fence. At two-thirty a taxi pulled up in front of the house.

"Hello, how are you?" said Marie as she stepped out. She was wearing a green blouse and slacks.

"Hi, Marie," said Tom. "Where have you been?"

"Swimming," answered Marie. "My sister takes me to a big pool to swim. I really like it but she won't get in the water. Then we go for ice-cream afterwards." She smiled. "Do you like to swim?"

"What are you doing here?" demanded Suzy, exiting the taxi with difficulty. "I told you not to come back."

"We need to talk," said Tom. "About your brother."

Both sisters immediately tensed. Marie's eyes looked watery; Suzy's were angry and hard. "Why can't you leave us alone?" Suzy snapped.

"I live in that house on Clendenan," said Tom. "We opened up a wall on the first floor, and inside…"

"Let's go in the house," Suzy announced. Marie and Tom followed her to the door. "Go get the iced tea, Marie," she ordered once they were inside. "Use the yellow glasses with the big flowers on them."

"I like those glasses," said Marie. "They're pretty. Yellow is my favorite color, after pink."

Suzy watched Marie walk down the hallway, then gestured for Tom to follow her into a starchy room that looked like an old-fashioned parlor. "What do you want?" she whispered. "We don't have much money."

"I'm not blackmailing you. I found a child's bones in my house and I want to know what happened. It wasn't the owners' child. So I started to look at who else had access to the house. Donald O'Neill was hired to do the repair work, and it was an extensive job."

"The house was gutted by that fire," Suzy sighed. "It took father ages."

"He was working on it for more than two years. That's a long time."

"It was a big job. Father had plenty of work, and some other jobs were more pressing."

"The bones I found were wrapped in newspaper from July 1945. That was while he was working on it."

Suzy sighed grimly, and her chin slumped. "It sounds like you already know what happened," she said, closing her eyes. "What more do you need to hear?"

"Your mother had a child, a baby boy, that May," said Tom. "Donald Alan O'Neill, Junior. There's a birth record but no death record. What happened to him?"

Marie came into the room, walking slowly. She'd filled the glasses to the brim and she watched them with wide eyes, clearly worried they might spill. "Careful now," she said to herself. "Careful." She smiled at them as she handed over the glasses.

"That's a good girl," said Suzy. "Thank you, Marie. Do you think you could check how many tins of fruit we have in the larder? I think we might make a fruit salad this afternoon."

"Oh, I love fruit salad!" Marie rushed out of the parlor.

"What happened to your brother?" Tom repeated.

Suzy took a sip of iced tea. "You can see that something's not quite right about my sister, can't you?"

"Yes," Tom said.

"She's been like that since she was born. She was fifteen before she could dress herself, and she still can't tie her own shoes." Suzy set her glass down. "It's been my job, my life, taking care of her. Our parents never wanted to put her in an institution. You can't imagine what a nightmare that would have been. The way they treated the retar... the way they treated people like Marie."

"I understand. But what about your brother?"

Suzy stared at the rug. "My brother was a colicky baby. Everyone tried to soothe him. Including Marie."

A picture was starting to form in Tom's mind. "What happened?"

"It was an accident," Suzy said. "He just slid out of her arms. It happened so fast." For a moment, the only sound was Marie's voice from the kitchen, counting in a singsong tone. "My parents were grief-stricken. They knew if anyone found out, Marie would be put into an institution. They couldn't let that happen."

"So your father took your brother's body and put it in the house."

"All I knew for certain was that he took Donny away. We were never allowed to talk about my brother, but sometimes I would listen at my parents' door, and I heard them talk about him."

"Someone could have found the body years before this."

Suzy shook her head. "But they didn't."

Tom was preoccupied when he got to the spa. Richard had said to be there at two, and it was almost four when Tom arrived. *What am I doing here?* he thought, walking towards its glass doors. *This is bullshit. Richard knows it.* Tom was already narrating the O'Neill sisters' story in his mind. They wouldn't want to do it, of course, but there was no reason for them not to. No one was going to put Marie in an institution for an accident that happened decades ago.

Tom was so focused on his story that he didn't recognize the woman who stepped out of the spa's front door. She was wearing a sundress and a pink cardigan and flip-flops, with she was still pulling her dark hair back in a ponytail. She stopped dead. "Tom?"

"Monica? What are you doing here? You're supposed to be in Montreal."

She fished in her bag for her sunglasses and put them on. "I came back this morning. I was going to surprise you. So much for that." Without kissing or touching him, she walked away.

Monica was in the bathroom, splashing around the clawfoot tub, when Tom came home that evening, He raised his fist to bang on the door. *What the hell is going on?* he wanted to demand. But he

Hilary Davidson

had little to go on except her inconsistent stories and a feeling of dread. He lowered his hand, and walked into her office.

The room, with its pale green walls and antique desk, was off-limits to Tom. I need space to work and I can't have you invading my space, Monica had told him. Her laptop was sitting on her desk and she'd left her e-mail logged on. He clicked on a message with the subject Can't wait.

Got the champagne. Can't wait to see you.

Tom's eyes burned. He clicked through a series of older messages from the same sender, a bundle of random letters and numbers at a Hotmail account. What hit Tom hardest was a message Monica had written a couple of weeks earlier.

The cat's away, it read. Come on over to play.

Tom stared at the time stamp. He'd had been away then, out of town covering some stupid comic-book conference. While he was gone, had Monica slept with another man in his own house?

"What are you doing?" snapped Monica from the doorway. She was wearing a short satin robe, and her hair was in a pink cotton towel swirled into a turban.

Tom stared at her. "You're having an affair."

It wasn't a question. The words hung between them for a moment, until Monica shrugged. "What the fuck did you expect?"

Later, when Tom tried to remember how things had turned out the way they had, all he could picture was Monica, standing there defiantly, not remorseful or sad. She was, if anything, angry at him. She'd stormed off to the bedroom, pulling on jeans and a T-shirt while Tom asked her why, why, why? He had stood there, tears welling, while she threw some clothing and jewelry into a bag. Then she'd grabbed her computer and stormed downstairs.

Just tell me, Tom had begged, grabbing her arm. How did it happen?

Easy, Monica had answered. Her eyes were shiny and her mouth was curled up at the corners, ready to shoot out something that would cut him to the quick. I met a real man who's not a pussy.

She tried to shove Tom away, but when he wouldn't let go, she scratched at his face, barely missing his eye. He shoved her back. Down she went, through the open doorway to the basement, the thudding of her body reverberating against the metal steps. Tom ran down after her, but she was gone, her empty eyes fixed on the ceiling.

Long into the night, Tom sat in the basement, picturing the house ablaze. He'd crossed Monica's arms over her chest. He should get her some flowers, he thought. He looked out the tiny casement window into the bleak backyard. It could have been beautiful if someone just planted flowers and took care of it. Now it was too late.

Early in the morning, Tom left a message on Richard's voice mail, saying he had to go to Vancouver because his mother was sick. His mother had died when he was a teenager, but Richard wouldn't know that. Then Tom went to the basement and started to dig. It was hard work, turning the earth, even though someone else had started the job. Tears and sweat stung his eyes. He thought about Marie O'Neill. How horrified she must have been when she realized she'd accidentally killed her baby brother. Somehow she'd lived with the pain, but Tom knew he couldn't.

After he buried his wife, Tom sat on the metal steps above her grave. He thought about staying there forever. Starving to death would be a painful way to go, exactly what he deserved. What would he tell Monica's mother? He was too ashamed to face anyone. He rested his forehead on the cool step and willed his heart to stop.

Instead, the doorbell rang. There was a pause and the bell sounded again. Go to hell, Tom thought, but next he heard the heavy front door swing open with its horrible squeal.

Tom moved up the stairs, into the kitchen. No one was there. He looked down the hallway and saw the front door was closed. Had he imagined it? No: there were footsteps above. Whoever it was that had broken into the house was upstairs. Tom pulled a serrated knife out of the wooden block on the counter. The footsteps were loud and heavy, pacing from room to room.

How many unexpected guests was he dealing with? Tom looked for a place to watch from, but the rooms on the first floor were virtually empty. There hadn't been money for the furniture Monica wanted. There weren't even drapes to hide behind. When he heard the heavy footsteps on the landing above the stairs, Tom ducked into the hole in the wall. The stink of mildew and mold hit him hard. Footfalls were coming down the stairs now. Someone passed in front of him and Tom saw black leather wingtips and black trousers. A bouquet of red roses obscured the face.

Roses? he thought. Had the man been pretending to deliver flowers when he broke in? But he was relieved that there was only one man. He'd take him on. It was as good a way to go as any.

He stepped out of the wall and padded down the hallway, glad he was barefoot. The intruder was peering into the basement, but he looked around when a floorboard squeaked under Tom's foot.

"Where are you hiding, you naughty little..." The words died on Richard's lips.

"I guess you're looking for my wife," Tom said. There was a feeling of calm that had come over him, as if this moment was suspended in time. The pieces of the puzzle suddenly fit. Monica had wanted to work in television, and Richard was a big-shot producer. Of course they'd been fucking around behind his back.

"You've got it all wrong," Richard said, his face pale and his eyes darted around the room.

"It's alright. Tell her I said hello." Tom thrust the knife up into the hollow of Richard's throat. Suddenly everything was slick and red: Richard's neck, Tom's arm, and the blade that connected them. Richard gurgled bloody bubbles and his eyes went wide. Tom shoved him hard and Richard sailed through the air. As he crashed down the metal steps, the red roses scattered and followed him into the dirt.

After Tom dug a grave for Richard, he washed in the clawfoot tub. Then he found Richard's car parked on the street, put the keys into the ignition and left the doors unlocked. Even with the gentrification of The Junction, it wouldn't take ten minutes for that car to be on the road, piloted by a kid who wouldn't believe his luck.

Back at the house, Tom picked up the phone and dialed.

"Hello?" The voice on the other end was suspicious.

"Suzy, it's Tom Lee again. We spoke yesterday."

"I wish you would stop hounding me, young man. We don't want any trouble."

"I wanted to tell you that I won't be bothering you again. What you told me was a confidence, and I intend to keep it between us."

"Well," said Suzy, her tone sharp. And then, softly, "Well, then."

"I apologize for bothering you in the first place," Tom said. "I'm sorry for making you rehash the past."

After he hung up, he sat lost in thought. He remembered how he and Monica used to stay up nights talking about how perfect they would make the house. It would never be what they had dreamed. It was a place of misery, where a fire had raged, a baby had been entombed, and his own wife had died. Yet, when he turned it over in his mind, he couldn't escape the conclusion that Monica had gotten what she deserved. Maybe he could've forgiven her if she'd been screwing someone else, but Richard? Never. For a moment, he wondered how the cellar door had opened just before she fell down the stairs. He didn't remember opening it. Had Monica turned the handle? Everything had happened so fast. Was it possible that it was some shift in the old bones of the house that caused the door to spring open? The house had its own secrets. It had kept the confidence of the O'Neill family for decades. How long would it take for...

The ringing phone made him jump.

"No one can make heads or tails of that poor wee babe you found," said Ramsay.

"Still going in circles?" asked Tom.

"I think they're giving up on it. Sorry about that."

"It's okay. Monica thought it would be a good story, but I'd just as soon leave it alone."

"Is she back yet?"

"No."

"Aww, chin up, lad. Look, she's being a spoiled little minx, wanting you to fix up the house for her. When you do, she'll be back."

"You think so?"

"I know so. Look, it's a big job, but you've got to start somewhere."

"The basement," said Tom. "Do you know anyone who could pour a concrete floor?"

HUNGRY HEART

Tommy flirted with the waitress for three weeks before she finally invited him back to her place. Her name was Liz and she worked at a diner outside Hellertown, PA, where Tommy was crashing for the summer. They'd been playing a little cat-and-mouse game since he'd first clapped eyes on her. Liz rebuffed his overtures a couple of times, but gently, on account of her kid. When he strolled into the diner that Thursday evening, he was half-worried that her brat would foul up their plans for the night. But then he saw Liz's wide mouth curve into a sly smile, and he knew he'd be going home with her.

She sauntered up to his table. Liz was a brunette with a thick mane of hair that cascaded around her shoulders and full breasts that threatened to pop out of her polyester uniform. He figured her for a knockout when she was younger, but youth had worn thin and she'd gone a little hard around the eyes. Not that he minded; he wasn't looking for a girlfriend, just a great screw.

"Feeling lucky, punk?" Her voice was a low growl.

"Hell, yeah."

"Jake's got an Iron Man marathon at his friend's house."

She said it like he should care about what her kid was doing. He didn't, but he grinned. "Great. What time do you get off?"

"Less than an hour."

"I guess I'll wait for you here." He'd already showered at the country club where he worked, and it wasn't like he wanted to go back to his motel room. The roaches didn't seem to mind his company, but he didn't care for theirs.

Liz smoothed the edge of his collar. "All dressed up. Now you got someplace to go."

Tommy smiled at that. He was wearing what he thought of as his work uniform. He'd lucked into a job at the Silver Creek Country Club, and even though he didn't know the first thing about golf, he had a talent for flattering the self-important. More importantly, he was a quiet purveyor of all the quasi-legal and downright illegal pharmaceuticals such gentlemen required as a balm for their inflated egos and saggy cocks. All of them had families they secretly hated—wives growing flabby, or else working out like maniacs so they could screw the pool boy— teenage kids who gave them no end of heartache, elderly parents who wouldn't shut up and die already. Tommy regarded them with a peculiar kind of horror. He'd been one of those losers once. He was lucky he'd gotten out alive.

"I'll get you some coffee," she offered.

As she moved off, his phone buzzed. It was a text from Carlos, a guy he'd known since forever. They'd lost touch when Tommy had spent a few years out in California. But life out west never matched the dream, and when Tommy returned to his old stomping grounds, he'd reached out. Carlos supplied good product, and Tommy's country club clients hoovered it down.

Can't make tomorrow, Carlos texted. But I can drop by right now.

Tommy glanced at his watch and groaned inwardly. Carlos could be such a pain in the balls. How far away are you? I'm at a diner. Tommy texted the address. He couldn't blow Carlos off. He'd get what he needed for the weekend and be done with it.

When Carlos walked in, they did their back-slapping bro-hug. "Sorry for the change of plans, man," Carlos said. "Marie's mom is sick, and I gotta…"

"Shit, that wife of yours has you locked down tighter than Fort Knox," Tommy said.

Carlos shrugged. "It's just one of those things."

Tommy snickered. "One of those things that says you're whipped."

"Yeah, well. You'd know how it goes if you'd stayed with your wife and kids."

"But I was smarter than that."

Liz dropped a menu on the table. "You want something to drink?" she asked Carlos.

"Coffee, please. No, wait." Carlos consulted his watch. "It's too late for caffeine. You have decaf?"

"No."

"Uh, just water, please."

Liz glanced at Tommy, as if to say Thanks for bringing your deadbeat friends in, buddy, before moving toward the water pitcher on the counter.

"You're not going to believe who I ran into," Carlos said.

"Who?"

"Ashley."

Tommy blinked at him, trying to remember an Ashley. There'd been so many girls over the years, he was sure there were a handful of Ashleys sprinkled in. "Ashley who?"

"You kidding me, man?" Carlos prompted. "Ashley, your daughter."

Tommy sat back and ran a hand through his hair. "Huh. She's got to be, what, fifteen or sixteen now?"

"Eighteen," Carlos corrected him.

"Whoa. Time flies."

"She looks a lot like your ex did at her age. A knockout, if you don't mind me saying so."

"Knock it off, man."

"What?"

"That's my kid you're talking about."

"Come on. You haven't seen her for a decade, Tommy. Kids grow up. You want to see a picture? It'll blow your mind, where I saw her."

"No, I don't," Tommy said quickly. "Look, I need to get out of here soon."

Carlos was clearly miffed, but they made their transaction, and he took off. Liz took her sweet time circling back to the table.

"You want to head out now?" Tommy asked.

There was a crease between Liz's eyes, like she was thinking hard. Too hard. "You didn't tell me you have a kid."

That caught Tommy by surprise. What business was it of hers if some of his DNA was out walking around?

"I don't. Not really."

"What does that mean?" Liz asked. "You either have a kid or you don't. It's not something you go halfway on."

"I broke up with their mom years ago. We're not in touch."

"Their mom?" Liz's tweezed eyebrows shot up. "There's more than one?"

Tommy didn't want to have this conversation. There was a boy and a girl and it had been forever since he'd tried to picture their faces. If he passed them on the street now, they'd be strangers. "Does it matter?"

Liz's eyes got flinty. "You know my scumbag ex walked out on me and Jake, right?"

"Okay…"

"You don't get it, do you?" She stared him down. "Why would I want anything to do with a pig who did to his own family what my ex did to me?"

She turned on her cheap heels and clattered off. He watched the back of her head and felt like punching it. Some used-up slop-server was going to cop an attitude with him? Well, fuck her.

He hit the john, locking the door and laying out a line of coke. That made him feel better for all of sixty seconds. He had a love-hate relationship with coke. The high was so brief and it left him all jumped up and buzzing afterwards.

He walked out without a word. Forget that stupid waitress, he'd find better action. He didn't want to hit anywhere in Hellerstown, because he couldn't afford to run into any of the creeps from the country club. So he drove aimlessly for a while, wishing he was back on his bike instead of a car. His ex-wife had made him give it up after he got into an accident with a tree, and he still resented the hell out of her for it. He should've bought another bike after he ditched her, he thought, but after he walked out, he'd given up on the idea of owning things. He never wanted to be tied down to anything again. He'd had enough of that life. He'd tried living it for eight years, and he'd hated it. Every day, he felt like something was dragging him down, and he knew he'd feel like that until the release of the grave. Something had to give. Caught between a rock and a hard place, he ran.

He cruised into Allentown, parking outside a dive bar. Inside, he planted himself next to a twenty-something girl who reminded him of Jennifer Beals in Flashdance.

"You know who you look like?" he asked her.

She didn't turn around.

He repeated himself.

She acted like she didn't hear him.

Stuck-up bitch, he thought. He left and walked a couple blocks to a bar that had some college kids in it. Now, these girls were hot. But they gave him strange looks when he tried to talk to them. Stuck up, that's what they were. Some guy walked up to a chick he was about to hone in on, a friendly looking girl with big tits. "Hey, Ashley," the guy said.

That hit Tommy like a hammer. Ashley? He had a fleeting vision of his little girl dressed in a tutu. He forced the memory into a box at the back of his brain, blaming Carlos for letting it escape. That wimp let his wife boss him around. Soccer games, ballet recitals, family dinners and Disney World trips. Tommy never put up with that shit. He was his own man.

He did another line of coke. All was right with the world for a moment, until he noticed his heart pounding. Was he having a heart attack? It was like even his own body was turning against him. When he was younger, he'd been able to party night after night. Now, the rush lasted about as long as a sneeze.

He drove aimlessly for a while, tasting bitterness. The truth was, as much as he insisted on having his freedom, the loneliness was hard to take. It was Liz's fault, he decided. That lousy cocktease had wrecked his night. Well, he'd teach her a lesson. He knew where she lived—a sloping house just off the 78 in the no man's land between Allentown and Hellertown.

When he pulled up in front of her place, he noticed her car parked out front. Maybe she'd had enough time to cool her heels? A guy could hope. He brushed off the front of his shirt and knocked on the door.

Liz opened the wooden front door

"Hey, babe," he said.

"I thought you might turn up." She left the storm door shut between them. "What d'you want?"

"That's no way to say hello."

"What part of fuck off don't you get?"

"You don't mean it."

"Beat it before I call the cops."

That was the last straw. "You bitch," he said, grabbing the handle of the storm door and wrenching it open. Liz tried to slam the heavier door, but Tommy rammed his shoulder against it. "You think you can invite me over and turn me away?" he demanded. "I don't…"

The gunshot filled his ears. His stomach was being squeezed in a vise and on fire at the same time. He reached forward to grab the gun away from Liz, but the pain forced him to stumble back, against the storm door. He fell to the ground.

"Don't worry, I'll call 911," Liz snarled. "Just as soon as you bleed out."

Images of his life started to swirl in front of Tommy's eyes, visions of a little girl dancing and a boy playing with Lego. Birthday parties and recitals and play dates. Then his wife's face floated past. He'd pushed it to the furthest reaches of his mind, but his ex was still in there, a ghost that would never die. He saw their tiny little wedding and the look on her face when she told him she was pregnant. He remembered what she'd looked like in high school, how he'd craved her like he'd never wanted anything in his life. He'd spent years running away from them, but these ghosts were soaked into the fiber of his being. He didn't exist without them.

Liz's harsh voice broke through his thoughts. She leaned forward, just a little, and her voice dropped to a hiss. "It's not like anyone's gonna miss you."

A HOPELESS CASE

Jump, Sarah ordered herself.

The number four express train was roaring towards the station. It was all of nine, maybe ten heartbeats away.

Jump. Jump. Jump. No more excuses. Time to jump.

She'd been mentally preparing for this moment for days, but now that the time to act was upon her, she hesitated, closing her eyes and taking a deep breath. When she fantasized about her death, it seemed so simple. She would fall forward in a gentle arc, like a scuba diver pushing one flippered foot off a pier, just as she and Colin had done countless times into the warm embrace of the Caribbean. She'd dive for the subway tracks, but be intercepted by the train. It would be a clean, swift meeting of flesh and metal with only one possible outcome.

No one else would be harmed. That was essential.

What Sarah hadn't envisioned, until she was standing on the platform, was the driver of the train. In her daydream, it was just a faceless, eyeless train. She saw herself being killed before anyone knew what had happened. She hadn't thought about the driver seeing her. A week earlier, when she'd been walking on the George Washington Bridge, looking for the right spot to leap from, she'd realized how impossible it would be to end her life there. Certainly, she would die, but before her body was cold, rescue workers would be dragged in. Sarah didn't want anyone else to be affected by her death. What if the subway driver saw her throw herself in front of the train? Would that person have nightmares for weeks or months or years to come, visions of a forty-five-year-old woman in a headscarf splattering before their eyes?

The train rushed past. Sarah opened her eyes and caught a silvery blur, before it screeched to a halt. She'd missed another chance. Her chest felt heavy yet hollow at the thought of returning to her empty little apartment.

"Ma'am?" Suddenly, there was a hand on her arm. Sarah turned her head, blinking in surprise. Beside her was a uniformed police officer, a thirtyish woman with her black hair pulled back a severe style that only emphasized the gentle roundness of her face.

"Yes?" Sarah whispered, unsure whether the other woman was part of a dream.

"Are you okay, ma'am?"

"I'm…" Sarah started to speak, but the doors of the train closed and it started to pull out of the station, screeching as it went. Her lips formed the words, "I'm fine," but the noise covered up her lie. How long had it been since she'd felt fine? It had been over a year since the bottom had fallen out of her world.

"You looked like you were about to fall off the platform," the officer said. "Like maybe you were having a dizzy spell. You feeling maybe a little lightheaded?"

"A little," Sarah repeated after her. It was as good an explanation as any. "Maybe a little."

"Okay, walk with me."

"Where?" Sarah asked, but she was already following. The woman was leading her by the hand, as if she were a kindergartener. Sarah was aware she'd developed such a suggestible personality since getting sick. Before the chemotherapy and the countless other meds had weakened her body and clouded her mind, she'd been another person altogether. Her mother used to describe her as ornery, like a horse that hadn't been broken.

They'd fought constantly, but Sarah missed her mother now that she was gone. It had been a decade since she'd passed, and even though Sarah knew it would earn her a smug I told you so, she wanted to tell her mother she'd been right about Colin Gratham when she'd called him a shameless, self-indulgent brat. After twenty years of marriage, Sarah had arrived at the same conclusion.

"Just over to the bench," the officer said, her voice placid, as if they were out at a park for a stroll. "I think you ought to rest your legs for a bit."

There was something southern in the lilt of the officer's voice, and Sarah let its gentleness lull her. She felt quietly placid, being led along like a lamb.

"This looks good." The cop gestured at a wooden bench and Sarah took a seat. The cop sat next to her, making a small sigh of pleasure, keeping up the pleasant companionability. Sarah kept her head down, worried what the cop might see in her face.

"I'm Elena, by the way. What's your name?" the cop asked.

Even though Sarah wanted to make something up, she said, "Sarah."

"That's a pretty headscarf."

"Thank you."

"You have cancer?" the cop asked. Her voice was gentle.

"Progressive multifocal leukoencephalopathy." Sarah's mouth felt tired reciting all those horrible, hateful syllables, but she read the incomprehension in the other woman's face. "I've been battling autoimmune diseases for a long time," she explained. "Then I suddenly started having neurological problems, too. Every treatment has failed. The last-ditch resort is chemo."

Elena nodded. "When I saw the scarf, I thought chemo. When my mama had it, she lost her hair, too. Even her eyebrows."

Sarah risked a tiny smile. At least she still had her eyebrows. "How long ago did she…" How long ago did she die, she wanted to ask, but her dry lips wouldn't form the words.

"That was six years ago. But it all grew back, you know. Just took some time."

It was on the tip of Sarah's tongue to say, *How could a dead woman's hair grow back?* Then she realized, the police officer's mother hadn't died. Her cancer must've gone into remission. Lucky woman, Sarah thought, suddenly envious. Her eyes were hot and watery, and she struggled to keep her composure. When Dr. Bob, who was an old family friend, told her she only had six months to live, Sarah had taken the news stoically. She'd already been through surgery and chemo and all of the other hellishness cancer had thrown her way. What she hadn't expected was her husband's reaction. She'd imagined him holding her when she shared the doctor's awful prediction. Instead, Colin had crossed his arms in front of his chest. *I can't take six more months of this,* he'd told her. *That's too much to ask of anyone.*

What do you want me to do? Sarah had asked him, frantic.

There are other options, Colin had said. *It would be so much easier. Think of all the suffering you'll avoid.*

I don't care about the pain, she'd cried.

Other people's suffering, he'd clarified. *Do you have any idea how hard it is to live with someone who's on the edge of death? How impossible it is to move forward with anything in your own life while you're waiting for them to die?*

The memory of his words still brought bile into her throat.

"It will get better, you know." The cop, Elena, brought her mind back into the present. She sounded so reassuring. Sarah wanted to believe her. But she could still hear Dr. Bob saying, I don't want to call this a hopeless case, but I'm so very sorry, Sarah.

Dr. Bob had shaken his head and started at his plump little hands. She knew it was all but over for her.

"No, it won't get better," Sarah blurted out.

"Why would you say a thing like that?" The cop's brown eyes were so warm. Sarah knew she didn't understand a thing. Elena would never comprehend what it was like to be married to a man who was impatient for her to die. Months ago, she'd put on a bathing suit and tried to join him in the hot tub on their back deck. What are you doing? he'd demanded. I just cleaned it, you know. As if his own wife were a plague rat that might infect him. Then Colin had rented a small apartment for Sarah near the hospital. He pretended to be thoughtful, but she realized he just wanted her out of their house. There was such coldness in him. When they'd married, Sarah had loved his chiseled looks and pale blue eyes. Now, he seemed like an iceberg to her. She saw him once a month, and he was always armed with materials from Dying With Dignity and the Neptune Society. She knew he was just counting the days until she died.

"I have only a few months left to live," Sarah said. "And I'm alone."

"No kids? No husband? What about a sibling?"

"I have a cousin. She's my best friend, and she's been wonderful. But she's gone through some terrible things herself and I hate to burden her." Sarah regarded Louise with such admiration. Louise had nursed her own husband through a short but brutal illness, burying him eight months ago. Sarah exhaled a long breath, feeling as if her chest was ready to collapse in on itself. How could you burden someone who's already been through the wringer? Louise was already a solid reservoir of support, dropping by for regular visits and bringing a steady supply of medical marijuana that Sarah appreciated and vitamins that Sarah didn't have the heart to tell her went straight into the garbage. Sarah had long since given up hope in the healing power of any pill. "I have maybe three more months to live. That's all I've got left."

"Okay, then why don't you use it?"

Sarah was expecting sympathy, not a challenge. "Excuse me?"

"Everybody gets only a finite amount of time here, you know. Look around you. Some people, walking around healthy, they might be gone in a week. They just don't know it. But you know. So use your time."

"To do what?"

"Whatever you want. Come on, there've got to be a million things you want to do, right? And you're not in a sickbed. You look good. If it weren't for your hair, I'd never have guessed you were sick." The cop smiled at her. "Come on, dream a bit. What do you want to do?"

"I always wanted to go to Italy," Sarah said. "Ever since I saw *A Room With a View*. That must sound so stupid."

"Why? Who wouldn't want to go to Italy? Seriously, think about it. Are you well enough to travel?"

"What do you mean?"

"Did your doctor ban you from flying? Are there treatments you have to hang around for?"

She tried to picture what Dr. Bob would say. Technically, he was Colin's friend, but she felt sympathy from him that she never got from her husband. Dr. Bob would understand her desire to go to Italy, she was sure. "No, nothing like that. It's just that my husband never wanted to go to Italy."

"Do you have the money to do it?"

Sarah stopped to consider that. She knew she did. Money was the one thing she had in abundance. She could go to Italy a dozen times, if only she had the time. It was just that Colin refused to travel anywhere that English wasn't the primary language. He'd never admit that, but after years together, she was well aware of his weaknesses. "Yes, but..."

"But nothing! I'm telling you, go to Italy. Enjoy yourself. Enjoy every day you have." Elena the cop gave her hand a gentle pat. "And don't put too much stock in what doctors say. They told my mama she'd be dead in a year. She said she's not dying, just so she can spite them."

Sarah nodded. The police officer's words reverberated in her head, knocking cobwebs out of the corners. What had she been thinking, letting her last days drag on in a tiny, airless apartment, tight with thoughts of death? Why wasn't she doing what she wanted to do? Whatever urge she'd felt to harm herself was gone now, extinguished like a flame deprived of oxygen. Why had she wanted to do something so foolish? It wasn't like her at all. Dr. Bob had prescribed an antidepressant for her that seemed to work in reverse; instead of lifting her up, it had dropped her in the gutter. *Just ride it out,* Bob had insisted. *Most antidepressants are tough to deal with for a couple of weeks, but when they kick in, they're miraculous.*

I'm still waiting for that miracle, she thought. And then she realized she'd found it. She felt buoyant suddenly, as if the antidepressant was finally doing its job. Three more months. That wasn't so terrible, was it? Elena was right. There were people with far less time than that, only they didn't know it.

She let Elena take her upstairs, through Grand Central's glorious main hall, and put her in a taxi on Forty-Second Street. She gave the driver the address of her rental on Amsterdam Avenue. When she got there, she stood in front of the building, thinking. She didn't want to go up to that horrible little apartment whose sole virtue was proximity to a cancer-treatment center.

Instead, she walked down the block to her parking garage, got her Lexus, and headed north, out of New York City and into the Hudson Valley.

Italy. What a beautiful, crazy, wondrous dream. She knew Colin would never approve, but that didn't matter. She had her own money, and she didn't need him to agree to anything. She'd go back to the house, pick up her passport and a few things, tie up any loose ends, and head to the airport. In the back of her mind, she could envision Italy so clearly. There were Rome's Spanish Steps and Florence's Duomo and Venice's St. Mark's Square. What she didn't see was herself coming home. What did that matter, anyway? Use the time you have left, she told herself. Use it well.

When she was almost in Tarrytown, she flipped open her phone. She knew it was illegal to make a call while driving, but she couldn't contain herself anymore, and she called Louise.

"I have the craziest idea," Sarah said when Louise picked up. "How would you like to come to Italy with me?"

There was a stunned silence on the other end, filled with a little splash of water, as if Louise were in the bath. "Italy?" Louise said. "Sarah, darling, what on earth…?"

"I'm sick of sitting around waiting to die. I've decided to make good use of whatever time I have left. And what I want to do is visit Italy."

"That's absolutely wonderful," Louise said. "That's the best idea I've ever heard."

"I was thinking we could go to Rome and Florence and Venice and everywhere else. A month, maybe."

"Darling, that would be amazing. But you know I don't have the money to do that kind of thing."

"Don't worry about that. I'll take care of everything. Just say you'll go with me."

"Oh, I don't know... I'd love to, but I'd feel like I was taking advantage of you. You don't need the poor relation tagging along."

"Please. I've never traveled anywhere by myself."

Louise sighed. "You're very persuasive. Okay, let's talk about this tomorrow. Shall we have lunch at your place? I'll pick up a guidebook or two on the way over."

"Why not now?" Sarah was almost breathless with excitement. I could come over..."

"I was just getting ready for bed. I have a bit of a headache." There was a brief pause. "Are you feeling quite all right, darling?" Louise's voice was tight with concern.

"I feel like I'm dreaming," Sarah admitted. "But it's been a long time since I felt this good. If it's a dream, I don't want it to end."

When she hung up, Sarah realized the only thing she wasn't looking forward to was telling Colin her news. She knew he'd stand in front of her, arms crossed, blocking her physically and mentally. She'd do anything to keep him from wrecking her plans. She could almost hear his voice, telling her exactly how stupid she was, and that only a fool would travel in her condition.

There were no lights on at the house when she pulled up in front of it. Maybe she could collect her passport and everything else she needed without encountering Colin? Could her luck be that good? There was no chance he was asleep—it was only eleven at night—but maybe he'd gone out of town. She had a sneaking suspicion that his little jaunts were more about securing female companionship than they were about business, but she didn't care. She got out of the car and let herself into the house.

When she got inside, she let her eyes adjust to the grey light instead of flipping the switch. Light might dispel the magic of the moment, and that was the last thing she wanted. Why had she ever agreed to move out? She knew the answer: she simply hadn't been up for a fight. Inside the grand foyer, her eyes settled on the crystal chandelier that had once been her mother's. She knelt down and felt the fine wool of the gorgeous carpet that had come from Turkey; she'd never been there, but she was glad to have something that had traveled so far. Her world had been too small for too long. Now that she was ready to fly, her chest swelled with happiness. She caught sight of herself in the beautiful gilded mirror that had been her grandmother's. It was just a dim reflection in the grey light, but it made her smile. She wasn't someone dying from a rare, incurable disease anymore. She was a woman ready for the adventure of a lifetime.

Then she heard laughter.

It came in little waves from the back of the house. Sarah stepped out of her shoes, half-suspecting she was about to meet a ghost in the near-darkness. But the patio light was on, and she realized the sound had floated in through the screen of the sliding door. Colin was in the hot tub, and he wasn't alone.

"Can you imagine her wanting me to go to Italy with her? I think she's lost her mind."

Sarah's breath caught in her chest as she recognized Louise's voice. Only, it wasn't the sweet, soothing tone she was used to, but something harsh, laced with contempt.

"She's grasping at straws," Colin answered. "With any luck, she'll be dead in a week."

"I don't think she will." Louise's tone was dark. "I think she's going to live forever. Like that awful old woman in Ethan Frome."

"Are you sure you've been giving her the right stuff?" Colin asked. "Because I don't get how she's still alive. The chemo drugs broke her down. Weed softens up her brain and makes her pliable. And the rest…"

"I know what I'm doing. This isn't my first rodeo, darling."

In her discombobulated state, Sarah couldn't quite process it all at first. Louise… had done this before? Was that how her husband had died?

"I ask her if she takes the vitamins, and she swears she does," Louise went on. "Either she's got the constitution of a horse or…" Louise paused and Sarah crept closer to the door, just in time to see Louise drain a crystal flute. It was from Sarah's own set of wedding china. Colin reached for a champagne bottle in a silver bucket and refilled the glass.

"Maybe it was a mistake to make her move out," Colin mused. "Everything would've been over long ago if she hadn't."

"Yes, but I wouldn't have been able to move in with you, darling," Louise cooed. "It was so depressing, being in that creepy little house in Queens."

Sarah stood in the kitchen, watching the two of them kiss. Waves of shock were coursing through her, and yet it was also like watching someone else solve a puzzle for you. Had they poisoned her? How long had the two of them been plotting and planning together?

"Bob doesn't think she can last much longer," Colin said.

Bob? Sarah thought. Dr. Bob, Colin's friend from Harvard? He was in on this, too? Sarah thought of all the sad looks that had passed over his long face over the past year whenever he'd delivered bad news to her. It was always, I'm so sorry to tell you this, Sarah, but… She'd never thought of going to another doctor. Who'd give her better care than Dr. Bob would?

"I'm just so sick of waiting," Louise whined. "This is taking forever. At least my pathetic excuse for a husband had the good grace to die quickly."

"Which is why we need to be careful," Colin said. "If Sarah died suddenly and I inherit her money and immediately marry you, that's going to look suspicious, especially with your own husband dead for only a few months."

"I know." Louise sounded petulant. "But waiting is driving me mad, darling."

"Well, we shouldn't have to wait too much longer. Bob prescribed an antidepressant that will make her suicidal. This Italy thing is just a crazy last-ditch fantasy. She'll probably jump out a window in the next day or two."

That was all Sarah could listen to. Her mind was humming with questions, neurons ping-ponging from timelines to jagged fragments of fact and half-remembered conversations. So many little things had seemed off, yet she'd never put it together. None of it matters anymore, she told herself. With surprisingly steady hands, Sarah picked up the radio from the counter. It was on a long extension cord, because Colin used to love bringing it outside and listening to music under the stars. Or maybe he only longed to drown Sarah out. She checked that it was plugged in. It was.

Both Colin and Louise half-turned when they heard the screen door slide open.

"I think you should know," Sarah said, stepping forward with the slow grace of a sleepwalker while they sat with slack jaws, "I've decided to go to Italy by myself."

She threw the radio into the hot tub. She imagined sparks flying from it like lightning bolts and spearing her faithless husband and cousin. But nothing like that happened. Louise shrieked and thrashed in the water, screeching, "Get it out! Get it out!" But Colin was calm, getting to his feet and shaking his head.

"You crazy bitch," he said. "You thought you could electrocute us? That only works if you complete the circuit…"

Louise screamed. She'd grabbed the radio, but instead of forcing it out of the water, she'd instantly become the conduit for the electric current. Her head snapped back, but she couldn't let go. Colin tried to knock the radio out of her hands, but the contact sent electricity coursing through him as well. The pair thrashed in the water, with Colin falling back and hitting his head, before disappearing under the surface of the water. Louise tumbled back into a seated position, eyes wide open but fixed on nothing. The radio floated out of her hands and bobbed on the surface of the water.

Sarah watched Louise's lifeless face, counting to a hundred, and then two hundred, while she waited for Colin to resurface. When his body failed to do that, she retreated into the house, leaving the screen open. Without turning on a light, she went upstairs, extracting her passport and some cash from the desk in her little den. She wouldn't pack anything, she decided. She could get whatever she needed when she landed in Rome.

When she slipped behind the wheel of her car, she looked at herself in the mirror and slipped off her headscarf. Her head was covered in pale fuzz like a peach or a newborn. How sick was she really? She had no idea anymore. Some of the autoimmune illnesses predated her marriage, so she knew it wasn't all a murderous mirage. But someone other than Dr. Bob would have to investigate that one day. She'd had enough of doctors and sickbeds for one lifetime. What would happen to her without needles injecting poison into her veins and drugs to cloud her mind?

"Enjoy yourself. Enjoy every day you have," she told her reflection.

She pulled out of the driveway and headed back to the highway. John F. Kennedy Airport was less than an hour away. For the first time in a long while, she had something to look forward to.

THE BARNACLE

Jess was washing bloodstains out of her husband's shirt when the police came knocking at her door. She cleaned her hands at the pitted porcelain sink while they beat an aggressive tattoo. Not again, she thought, avoiding her own eyes in the scratched cabinet mirror. Twenty-seven and pregnant by a man who couldn't hold down a straight job, that was the truth of her life.

"Bobby Torres?" called out one of the cops. Jess went to the door and unlocked it.

"Good afternoon, officers. Can I help you?" In her words she heard the echo of her grandmother's voice, the lady-of-the-manor routine that was dusted off whenever the Belfast police came looking for Jess's father.

"Jessamine Murphy? Detective Hayden. My partner, Detective Roop. Can we come in?" the taller one asked. His craggy face was stretched funhouse-long. The squat man beside him could have escaped from the same circus, with a square head atop a round torso. His rubbery lips twisted from a sneer to a leer as he noticed Jess's cleavage. She pulled her silky robe closed.

"This isn't a good time," she said, her voice hinting at an Irish accent. Her roots always showed when she got nervous. "Bobby isn't here."

"When did you last see him?"

Jess paused before answering. It was never a good idea to give the police a straight answer; who knew how that might screw up an alibi later?

"Just a little while ago," Jess said. "But why would you be asking that?"

"What does 'a little while' mean?" the cop prodded.

"Really, officer, I think it's time you explained what you're doing at my door."

Roop chimed in. "Bobby Torres's car was found early this morning under the Williamsburg Bridge and the FDR. Someone set it on fire."

"Someone… what?" Jess was stunned, and she didn't try to hide it.

"It's worse than that. There was a body inside." Hayden paused for that to register. "Male. Shot in the head."

Jess's mouth fell open. Please, God, don't let it be Bobby, she prayed. "Do you know who…?"

"He's missing his face as well as his fingers and teeth, so we're having trouble ID'ing him." Hayden's voice was taut.

Jess's knees went wobbly at that. "What a terrible thing," she said. With her accent, it came out Whut uh terrbel ting.

"You can see why we need to know when you last saw your boyfriend. If it was this morning, we can rule out the possibility that the body is his."

"Husband," Jess corrected him.

Hayden's beady eyes blinked. "When did you last see him?"

I'm not sure," she hedged. "Bobby came home last night, but he was gone before I woke this morning."

"We'd like to come in, wait for your common-law husband," Roop said, larding the last few words with sarcasm. "Given Bobby Torres's history, I doubt that he was the man we found. More like the guy who'd chop off the fingers and…"

"That's enough," Hayden interrupted his partner, but the damage was done. Roop's implication couldn't be more clear.

Bobby had once been arrested for murder, but the case had never made it to court.

"You're welcome to wait in the hallway," Jess answered. She shut the door and turned all three locks before running back to the bathroom and throwing up. Bobby Torres's car was found early this morning... But Bobby had been in the apartment early that morning. He'd gone out a little before six a.m., she was certain, even though he'd tiptoed around the apartment and locked the door behind him with a barely perceptible click. But what did early mean to the cops? She cursed herself for not asking. Six? Seven? An hour could make all the difference in the world.

Pulling herself together, Jess brushed her teeth and splashed water on her face. It's not Bobby, she repeated to herself, and she decided that she was going to believe that. She examined the shirt and noted that the border of the bloodstain was still visible. Damn it, blood was hard to get out. She went to the window that overlooked First Avenue. Four stories down was a parked police car with two uniformed cops standing on the pavement. They were talking with the taller detective. There was no doubt they believed Bobby had killed that man. The police believed he was alive, too. That was bad, yet reassuring at the same time to Jess.

Jess went back into the bathroom, untied her belt and hung the robe up on the back of the door. She was wearing a lacy black bra and panties and she pulled the shirt over her. It fit in the arms but billowed around her narrow waist. She was three months along and her body had yet to make visible accommodations for the baby, though her breasts were already swelling. At this point, she could land a job at Scores, she thought. She wrapped the damp shirt around her shivering body. In the main room she sat on the unmade bed to pull on a pair of black tights before stepping into

Bobby's trousers. He was five-ten, a couple of inches taller than Jess, and from a fashion perspective it was horrible. But from a get-the-evidence-out-of-the-apartment perspective, it wasn't bad at all. She sat down to put on her wedge-heeled black boots, then pulled a black wrap dress over the ensemble and tied it at the waist. The dress-over-trousers look was something she'd seen on a makeover show on television, and maybe it worked for stick figures. On Jess's hourglass shape, it looked ridiculous. A bag of rags, her grandmother would have scolded. Still, under her winter coat, no one would be able to tell the difference.

The hardest thing to get rid of would be the gun. She was certain she'd find one. The handguns Bobby kept in a cereal boxes and a hamper were gone, as was the sheaf of old photos he hoarded in his dresser drawer. That was a little odd, she thought, wondering what else was missing. When she opened up the toilet tank, she found a revolver taped under the cover. She pushed away an image of a charred, mutilated husk of a man in Bobby's car as she got her dishwashing gloves from the kitchen sink and a clear plastic bag from the cupboard and went back to the gun. She freed it from the tape and slid it into the bag. The she grabbed her handbag, dumped it on the bed, and lifted its false bottom. This bag was her companion on shoplifting trips, but Jess hadn't used it to smuggle anything out of the apartment before. In went the gun and the balled-up wad of grey tape. She didn't think that the cops would be able to keep her from walking out of the apartment with the bag. Just try to take a woman's purse away from her, coppers.

She called Bobby's cell and got his voice mail. "Darling, the police are here at the apartment, they want to talk to you about a shooting, a man who was found in your car. I love you." She went through the apartment quickly, intending to collect her small cache of real jewelry, keys to safety deposit boxes, a modest roll of cash, and a collection of ready-to-be-issued counterfeit passports. That was all she had for a life, she thought, a few trinkets to be dropped into a bag; everything else had been left behind years ago. But those things were already gone. Bobby must've taken them when he'd gone out; it could only have been him. What was going on? A chill ran through her as she considered the possibility of a debt she hadn't been told about, or a job that had gone sideways somehow. It wasn't impossible that the body found in the car was...

No. She couldn't let herself think that, not for a second. She had to survive, and the only way to do that was to keep swimming forward, away from the cops and other predators who would try to bring her and Bobby down. From under the sink she grabbed several bottles of extra-strength drain cleanser. She poured one down the kitchen drain, then equal measures down the shower and the cracked sink.

As she pulled on her black wool coat, she had a thought. She got a blue shirt of Bobby's out of the hamper and put it in a plastic shopping bag. Pleased with herself, she opened the door to the hallway and locked it behind her. She took the stairs down because the rickety elevator rarely worked, and even when it did Jess was terrified of getting stuck in it. She went out the back way, and there was Detective Roop, waiting for her, the sneaky thick bastard.

"Going somewhere, Miss Murphy?" he sneered.

"Doctor's appointment."

"What's in the bag?"

"Just a shirt for the dry cleaner's."

"Let me see," he said. Jess made a show of reluctance, and then handed it over. He looked inside and cocked his head. "Was this what your husband was wearing last night?"

"No," said Jess. "It's been in the laundry bin for ages."

He looked at her, and she knew he'd swallowed the bait. With every bit of dignity she could muster, she turned and walked down the alleyway, shivering as the chill January wind hit her face.

She circled the Goodwill on East Twenty-Third Street a couple of times to make sure no one was following her. Then, in a curtained cubicle, she discreetly shed Bobby's shirt and pants onto hangers, which she tucked onto the appropriate racks. No other man would look as fine in those clothes as Bobby did, she was sure. Her husband was thirty-five and strikingly handsome, a wall of muscle sharply defined by long hours in gyms both in and out of prison.

Jess got a little dizzy as she went out to the street again. She hadn't had a bout of morning sickness until this very morning, and she put this new complication down to nerves. She was vulnerable in new ways since she'd become pregnant. Sounds were louder, tastes sharper, and smells were overwhelming. She knew exactly when the people who lived down the hall lit up a joint, or what all the neighbors were having for dinner on any given night. Walking on a crowded street was starting to get difficult for her. She caught the scent of souring perfumes and exhaled smoke, mingled with notes of urine. She was fervently glad it was winter, and she didn't know how she would survive spring in this state.

It was a bitterly cold day, and at Union Square Jess went into the big bookstore at the north end and headed up the escalator and into the children's section. She ran her hands over the shiny, colorful books, the impulse to pop a couple into her bag almost irresistible. A counselor at the group home Jess had lived in when she was sixteen had told her that she took things to get back at the world, that it was a form of revenge. Jess had always thought that particularly stupid. What were things to her? She'd had to up and leave everything she owned behind more times than she could count. No, that wasn't true, she probably could count them. The first time was when her grandmother tossed her over the Atlantic, sending her into the care of a cousin in Rochester. She'd run away from that hellhole four times before she'd been put into a group home. That place was almost as bad as the cousin's, and she'd run away again. That was when she'd met Bobby, and when things had started looking up.

And soon baby would make three, Jess thought. While she waited for Bobby to call she picked through some pregnancy books, which thrilled and terrified her. There were so many things to be wary of, things she'd never dreamed would hurt a baby. Fresh vegetables, for instance. Who would have thought of that as anything but healthy? But no, a bit of contaminated spinach or lettuce could kill the child. Jess had made Bobby swear to clean up his act when she found out she was pregnant. No more cigarettes, booze, and Chinese takeout. No shouting, not even at the television, not even if the Rangers were down in the third period. He hadn't liked it, not one bit, and he'd made a terrible joke about her getting rid of the baby that had upset Jess for a week before he finally convinced her he hadn't meant it, not really. "Stupid barnacle," he'd muttered, but he'd smiled when he'd said it.

But she hadn't said a word to him about his questionable business activities. Money had to come from somewhere, after all. But now she was getting frantic. Where was he, and why hadn't he called? Surely he wouldn't have been foolish enough to go home, not when she'd warned him about the police? In the back of her mind was the ugly, nagging suspicion that maybe that body in the car could be… No! Don't think like that. Believe in Bobby. He's fine. He has to be.

She wandered by the café on the third floor. Look at that, she thought, seeing a man get up, leaving his cell phone on the table. By the time he came back a moment later it was gone. Jess didn't want to tie up her own phone and run down the battery, in case Bobby called, but she needed to talk to the people he knew. Up on the quiet fourth floor of the store she made call after call. Nobody knew where he was, or so they claimed. Finally she ran out of numbers. She deleted the calls she'd made from the phone's log, then took the escalator down. "Someone must have dropped this," she told the clerk at the customer service desk, handing over the phone.

She left the store, facing the cold wind cutting across Union Square and found a health-food store on its eastern edge. She bought a protein bar and circled the park as she ate it, passing Gandhi's statue twice as she thought of whether she was supposed to dump the gun. She walked west, through the comparatively empty cross-streets of Chelsea. Here, she thought, she could take a chance and slip it into a concrete planter. Someone would find the gun and take it home, wouldn't they?

In desperation, Jess walked further west to the Hudson River. Bobby knew a lot of people who worked over there, shifty-eyed fences and swift-handed grifters, but no one she talked to had seen him. She could have wept with frustration. She was cold, she was hungry, and she needed to go to the bathroom for the tenth time that day. How much longer was she going to have to wander around the city? A fine thing this was to do to the mother of your unborn child, she wanted to tell Bobby. Make her run around like a rat in a maze until she dropped. Anger was better than fear, which had started to take hold of her mind. Where the hell was he? Tears squeezed out of the corners of her eyes but she told herself that it was because of the bitter wind.

The temperature had dropped several degrees, and the night chill hurried her along the streets. It was a Monday, and she wasn't sure if it was the cold that kept people in, or if it was just too early in the evening for much to be going on. She walked along Delancey Street to the mouth of the Williamsburg Bridge, looking for a burned-up car or chalked-up pavement, but the police must have carted the crime scene away. Where else was there to look? Bobby liked to hang out on the Lower East Side, but she doubted she'd find him wandering its streets that night. He was in hiding, he had to be, that much was clear to her now. Still, she paced block after block, taking in the old synagogue and the new glass hotel and everything in between. At Suffolk Street she stopped dead. Gates of Hell read a scarlet neon sign a couple of blocks down.

Jess had never been to the club, but she knew about it. Bernardo Diaz, an old pal of Bobby's, owned it. But Bobby didn't like Jess going to clubs with him—he got jealous when other men eyed her—so she'd never been inside, even though Bernardo called her every week, asking her to come in. Now, she was drawn to it, as if by a magnet. She walked along Suffolk until she was standing under the neon sign. There were gargoyles peering down at her, eyes bulging and tongues lolling. They weren't any harder on the eyes than Detective Roop had been, she decided, reaching for the handle on the door. It didn't budge. She rapped at the opaque glass and stepped back. There was a rattle behind the door and it opened slightly.

"We're not opening tonight," said a beautiful wide-eyed blonde girl with a haughty expression. She was wearing a red headband with sequin-studded horns.

"I'm Jess. Is Bernardo here? Or, by any chance, has Bobby Torres stopped by?"

"Oh, are you one of Bobby's cousins?" asked the horned girl. The mention of Bobby's name made the girl smile and she opened the door wider. Jess could see that she was wearing a strapless red bodysuit, black fishnet stockings, and vertigo-inducing stilettos. It was almost like a Playboy bunny outfit except for the color and the wiry, barbed tail. "Come on in," the woman said. "It's so cold today."

Inside there were spotlights shining on murals of people roasting in cauldrons. The red velvet settees and gilded columns that could have come from a Victorian brothel, and an undulating black bar that snaked along one wall. "It was Bernardo's idea, making the club look like hell – literally, I mean." The blonde kept talking but all that stuck in Jess's mind was Cousin? Bobby had a lot of cousins, but none with her name.

"Why did you think I'm Bobby's cousin?" she asked.

"He has so many," the blonde answered. "I've only met a few of them. But I remember him mentioning that his cousin Jess was staying with him a few weeks ago. You don't look anything like him, you know."

Jess was speechless. Before she could find her tongue, a deep rasp of voice filled the room. "Jessamine."

Jess turned. The man standing there was Bobby's height but older, with a swollen stomach spilling over his belt and a cigarette dangling from his lip. He was wearing a dark suit and a white shirt without a tie. His cologne was expensive but it smelled to Jess as if he had spilled it on himself. She hoped the fresh wave of nausea would pass quickly.

"Hello, Bernardo," Jess answered. "How are you?"

"Better, now that I get to see you, babe." He moved toward her, pulling her into and hug and kissing her on each cheek. "Beautiful, just beautiful, as always." Jess wasn't certain what she found more sickening: the smell of him or the way he rubbed up against her every time she saw him. Fortunately, those occasions were rare.

"You have my money, boss?" the blonde interrupted.

"Don't show up here looking for an extra shift again, Lita," he answered, handing the woman some crumpled bills.

The woman's horns seemed to droop. "But Bobby said…"

"Screw Bobby. You're not going to be seeing him around here anymore. You do what I tell you."

"Sorry," Lita said meekly.

"Now get out," said Bernardo.

Lita walked behind the bar and grabbed a silvery coat. She put it on and tied the belt. The barb of her tail drooped just below the hem. "Okay," said Lita. She glanced at Jess. "Sorry, I meant to get you a drink. We do a really great cocktail we call the Hellfire…"

It was on the tip of Jess's lip to say that she was pregnant, but Bernardo spoke first. "You need me to tell you twice?"

"Thanks anyway," said Jess.

Lita nodded at her, walked to the front door, and let it slam behind her.

Bernardo moved towards her. His nose was thick with scar tissue, like a boxer's. His cheeks were pitted with acne scars and his eyes were hooded. "I'm kind of surprised to see you here tonight, Jessamine," he said, drawing out each syllable of her name as if he were tasting it. It was just one of the many reasons he made her flesh crawl. "What with everything going on."

"What, the dead body and the car?" Jess demanded. "I have a few questions for you about that."

Bernardo dropped his cigarette on the floor and crushed it, immediately pulling a gold case and lighter out of his pocket and lighting up again. His flabby jaw was tense. "Bobby's left us in a tight spot."

"What are you talking about?"

Bernardo's eyes flicked up at hers, then back down to her breasts. The wraparound dress gaped wide over the valley of her cleavage. "How about that drink?" he said suddenly, licking his lips. He went behind the bar and pulled out a bottle and two glasses. "You like scotch?" He poured some scotch into the glass and knocked it back like a shot.

"Not so much," said Jess. "Do you have any orange juice?" She shuddered at what the wafting smoke would do to her unborn child, but she forced herself to step closer to Bernardo and plant herself on a cushioned red barstool so that her chest was right under his nose. Bernardo got a carton of orange juice from a fridge beneath the bar and poured it for her. He smiled as he put the glass in front of her. His teeth were movie-star white and even. On a plain man, they would have enhanced his appearance, Jess thought, but on someone as troll-like as Bernardo they highlighted his hideousness.

"You always look so good, Jessamine," he said while she took a sip.

"Thanks," she muttered, thinking yuck.

"The fact you showed up here..." Bernardo was studying her face instead of her cleavage for once.

"What is it?"

"I told Bobby a while back you should come work at the club. Not work the floor like the other girls, but in the office with me, maybe. You like the place?"

Jess looked around, taking in every tawdry detail. It was clear that Bernardo had poured plenty of time, money, and effort into it, and painfully obvious that the man had no taste.

"It's like nothing else on Earth."

"Pure class," said Bernardo, removing the cigarette from his mouth only long enough to take another belt of scotch, then dragging hard again. "You should come work for me. You'd fit in here perfect."

"I don't think so." Work for a leering Bernardo? She was ready to throw up again.

"Well, you're going to need some kind of job now," he said.

Jess stared at him.

"With Bobby being gone, I mean."

Gone. The word hit Jess like a punch in the stomach. She fought to keep herself steady.

"Gone where?" she hissed.

Bernardo's eyes narrowed. "Down to Mexico."

You lying piece of trash, Jess wanted to say. But her mouth was dry. Bernardo's soulless black eyes were staring into hers now.

"Mexico's what he said, but who knows? He wanted to make a fresh start. Said he had too many problems. Told me I had to take care of you for him. Said he figured I'd been angling for that job for a while."

He picked up her hand and she recoiled. There's a gun in my purse, she reminded herself. I can use that if I need to.

"Keep your hands off me."

"You're gonna change your tune real soon." There was triumph in Bernardo's eyes, satisfaction and something greedy staring back at her. "I like your accent. That whole Irish thing is so sexy." She hadn't even noticed her voice betraying her. He looked her over as if he were assigning a price on her. "Can I ask you something? You're Catholic, right? Bobby told me he was the only guy you've ever been with. That true?"

"Yes," she said. "To both questions." She'd told Bobby that a long time ago. It wasn't as if she'd chosen anyone else before him. The cousin, the group home, well, that was just survival.

Bernardo smiled. "You're the old-fashioned type, aren't you? Most girls these days don't have much in the way of morals." He took another belt of scotch and lit another cigarette. "But I think you're also a smart girl. Sometimes it's time to move on."

"Move on?" said Jess, in a crackling whisper. She swallowed hard. "Could I use your bathroom?"

"You're not thinking about walking outta here, are you? We got a few things to get straight, now that Bobby's out of the picture." Bernardo's voice was hard.

She couldn't say a word as she stood. Her legs were shaky as she stepped across the floor, unsure where she was going

"It's that way," Bernardo called. In a mirror, she saw him pointing to a dark corridor.

Jess pushed the door open with her shoulder. The bathroom was lit with a red light, giving it an otherworldly glow. She looked at herself in the mirror over the sink. She knew without hearing the words that Bobby was dead and that Bernardo had killed him. This story he'd cooked up about Bobby needing to get away from New York was a pathetic lie. Bernardo had drooled over her every time she encountered him. He'd even sent her flowers. He killed Bobby because of me, Jess thought suddenly.

Bernardo is so evil he thought he'd get rid of Bobby and that I'd fall into his lap. The thought of sleeping with a sweaty, shifty Bernardo at any time repulsed her, but now that she realized what he'd done to Bobby, she was filled with rage.

Then she remembered the gun.

She opened up her black bag and—not worrying about gloves this time—took the gun out from under the false bottom. It was loaded. She cocked it and visualized shooting Bernardo's brains out of his skull. He deserved a slow, torturous death that would take days, but swift justice was all she'd be able to obtain for Bobby now. A wave of nausea hit her and she pressed her head against the cold tile of the wall.

What will happen to the baby? she wondered. Could she get away and make some kind of new life for them both? She felt a terrible sorrow for the child in her womb, knowing it would grow up now without a father. Jess started to sob. She'd lost her parents early on; at least she'd had her grandmother, for a time, but when Nana had gotten sick and shipped her over the Atlantic, Jess had been cast drift. She had no family to hold to, except for a cousin who'd wanted to use and abuse her. If she went to jail, her child would be taken away from her and would grow up in foster care. She stood there, gasping, trying to weigh the options. Run away and keep her child safe? Or exact justice for Bobby? She'd just made up her mind when she heard a shot.

For a split second, she thought it had come from her own gun, but the revolver rested quietly in her hand while a man screamed out. She cracked the door open and heard a voice. Bobby? It didn't seem possible. Jess opened the door and crept along the dark hallway.

"It know you've got money stashed somewhere, and unless you tell me where it is you're going to look like a piece of Swiss cheese."

That was Bobby. Her heart pounded in disbelief.

"You bastard," Bernardo said. "I paid you everything I owed you. You told me you were leaving town. Then you killed Eduardo and left him in your car. Why?"

"There's no other way the police would believe I'm dead," Bobby answered. "But, you know what? A new life—and a new identity—costs money. Even in Mexico. And when I started counting up what I got, I saw it wasn't enough. So I need your rainy-day fund now, buddy. Tell me where it is, or your other leg gets a bullet, too."

"Drop dead," Bernardo said. "I can't believe I was so stupid. You telling me you were done with Jess, how you even hated the sound of her voice now. How you wanted me to have her 'cause I'd take good care of her. I never should've believed you. Bastard, you know I been in love with her since I first laid eyes on her. I'm so stupid, I believed she came here tonight 'cause she was looking for you. I should've known you sent her in here to distract me."

"What the hell? The Barnacle was here? When?" Bobby sounded rattled.

"Like you don't know."

"I'm right here, Bobby!" Jess called, her voice trilling with excitement as she rounded the corner. Bobby was as handsome as ever, but his eyes were round with shock. He was standing over Bernardo, .38 in hand, while Bernardo sat on the ground, holding one leg, grimacing in pain.

"Jess." Bobby's voice was flat. His mouth moved again but nothing came out.

"I was so worried about you, Bobby! I'd started to think you were dead." She stepped towards him and his hand went up, leveling the gun at her chest.

"Get out!" he snapped.

"Bobby?" she said, stepping closer.

"I don't want to shoot you, Jess, but if that's what I have to do to get rid of you, I will. You're like some kind of sea monster that clings to its prey until it dies."

"But we're having a baby together," Jess whispered. "I love you and you love me."

"See, that's the thing. I'm tired of playing house," Bobby said. "It was never really my thing. But having a kid? Definitely not my thing. Remember me telling you to get rid of it?"

"That was just nerves talking. You'll love the baby when you meet him—or her. I know it."

"That's your insane fantasy talking, Jess. I'm walking out of here and going to Mexico and you are sure as hell not coming along for the ride."

"But… I love you. You can't leave me." Without thinking about it, she raised the gun. Bobby hadn't seen it because the billowing sleeve of her coat hid it.

"Put that down, Jess."

"Take me with you."

"Don't make me shoot you," he said. "I don't want to, but if it's the only way I can get rid of you, I will."

"You can't abandon me," Jess whispered. "I won't let you walk out of here without me."

Bobby turned the gun on her but she got the first shot off. There was an explosion of red on his white shirt, with streaks of blood blooming like the petals of a carnation. He fired a fraction of a second after Bernardo grabbed his arm, grounding the shot in the floor in front of Jess's boot. Bernardo pulled him to the ground and the gun out of his hand. Bobby touched the wound and stared at his hand.

"All I wanted was to get away," he murmured. "Just… away."

His eyelids fluttered and her slumped to the ground.

"Did I… did I kill him?" Jess asked.

"No, Jessamine. It's okay. Gimme the gun."

Without thinking, she handed it over to Bernardo. "He never wanted the baby. I tried to pretend that everything would be all right but…" She trailed off, staring at Bobby.

Bernardo pulled out his cell phone, dialed, and told someone to come over to take care of a deadbeat, that he needed a doctor for his leg, and he needed a driver to take his girlfriend back to his house. Girlfriend? "Don't worry. He's already off on a dirt nap," he added before he hung up.

"Is Bobby dead?" Jess asked him. From where she stood, Bobby didn't seem to be breathing. "I couldn't live with myself if I…"

"He's fine," said Bernardo. "This is gonna blow over, okay? Trust me."

The guilt crushing her chest started to lift. "Okay." If Bernardo said Bobby was fine, who was she to doubt him? She knelt down on the floor next to him. He was clearly in a lot of pain, but he asked, "You okay? You didn't get hurt, did you?"

"I'm fine." There was something oddly touching about his concern. Bernardo looked different to her now. Not ugly, but tough. Not fat, but solid. It was as if he were shifting before her eyes, taking on a different shape.

"My friend will be here in a few minutes, and he's gonna help me clean all this up. Just leave everything to me, will you?"

"Okay." She rested her head on his shoulder. It felt natural, somehow, as if she'd finally found the place she was supposed to be.

MY SWEET ANGEL OF DEATH

When I bought my one-way ticket to South America, it was with the intention of escaping everyone I knew. I spent twelve hours flying from New York to Lima to Santiago, then another hour on a crowded puddle-jumper to La Serena, a small, colonial city in northern Chile. Prescription pills kept me mercifully unawares on the first flight, but on the second I was squashed between a sharp-elbowed Englishwoman who hogged the armrest and a Chilean man in his late fifties who wheezed heavily while studying yellowed newspaper clippings. I didn't understand much Spanish, but even I could comprehend Niñas Perdidas hovering over photographs of sweetly innocent round-faced young girls. The man's intensity as he studied them made me edge away in my seat, even as the hawk-nosed woman jabbed at my ribs with increasing ferocity. Lost girls. It was the last story I wanted to see. I could barely comprehend my own losses, never mind taking in anyone else's. I shut my eyes and ears and swallowed another pill.

The ride from the airport was a different sort of terror, but at least it provided a distraction. Three hours in an all-terrain jeep barreling up, down and around the Cordera—the foothills of the mountains—making me grab the dashboard in front of me at every hairpin turn. "Muy bonita!" the driver called out, gesturing grandly with one arm at the olive groves outside La Serena. Later he repeated the gesture at the oddly green hills, virtually free of plant life but rich with copper.

Our destination was a hacienda tucked into a hillside midway down a river valley, a setting as tranquil and remote as its website promised. There were only five guestrooms, and when I arrived early in the evening, I met Benita and Miguel, the couple who owned and ran the place, and an elderly but spry German pair who were in for a repeat visit. They shared a love of horses that let them converse easily at dinner in the hacienda's terracotta-tiled dining room while I sat quietly. "Vegetarian, por favor," I muttered at the onset of the meal. Benita conferred with the cook, a squat, kindly woman who took one appraising look at me and smiled knowingly. I think she saw a type – high-maintenance, fat-phobic American woman – but eating even a few mouthfuls of soup and salad was a challenge for me. My appetite had vanished after the accident, and even though doctors had promised it would return, two years later, it hadn't. I didn't sleep that night until I broke out my little blue pills. I counted them carefully, tempted to take a handful. But I couldn't. I'd made a promise to my husband, after all.

I dozed through the next morning, jolting awake at intervals and staring at bright ochre walls before remembering where I was and letting myself slip back into a chemically induced haze. Around one o'clock, I got up and splashed cold water on my face, pulled on a T-shirt and jeans, and walked along the veranda to the dining room. Benita greeted me in excited, rapid-fire Spanish that I could only nod at. The cook brought out an avocado salad as I slid into a chair at the big wooden table. Almost immediately a strong pair of hands landed on my shoulders, making me jump. I hit the table and knocked over a pitcher of water.

"Gotcha," said a man with a deep voice.

I half-turned, trying to catch my breath. A man stared at me with blue choirboy eyes. He was six feet tall and blond, with glossy white on display as he grinned at me. "Don't touch me!" I hissed.

"Whoa, there, honey." He put his hands up in mock-surrender. "I didn't mean to ruffle your feathers."

I didn't know how to respond, so I was glad when Benita came over and fussed over the mess I'd made. The man pulled out the chair next to mine. "It's good to meet you. I'm Brian Lucas." He put out his hand and smiled expectantly.

"Don't ever do that again." I sounded humorless, but I didn't care.

"Aw, come on. It's a great story for the folks back home – one of Brian Lucas's famous practical jokes."

I've always been wary of people who talk about themselves in the third person. It's as if they don't know they're in the same room as their audience. "Do I know you?"

"'Course you do. You seen 'All Our Tomorrows'? I was on that for two years."

I didn't know what that was, but it sounded like a soap opera. Whatever curiosity I had vanished and I turned back to my salad.

"Don't you watch television?" He sounded a little desperate.

"Not shows like that."

"Oh, snooty. Well, I'm moving to the big screen anyway. I'm in that Wild West movie Coppola's directing. Or I will be when I learn to ride a horse. That's what brought me down here. I got a week to saddle up and learn the ropes. Though I've got time for other things, too."

I took a small bite of my salad and chewed thoughtfully. "I came here for the quiet."

Brian chuckled in a faux-hearty way to suggest he was unfazed. "You haven't even told me your name."

"No, I haven't."

He waited a beat. "So, what is it?"

At that moment, I realized I'd made a mistake. For all my careful planning to get away from everything, I'd booked the reservation with my real name. I hadn't been worried about Chilean people figuring out who I was. A few depressing news stories didn't make me an international celebrity. But a tragedy vulture had put my family on television for those who enjoyed gawking at misery. Google my name and you'd stand a good chance of finding footage of me weeping at my daughters' gravesite.

"Audrey." No surname required.

"Mmm. Like Audrey Hepburn. You even look like her."

I'd overestimated him. My name didn't matter. I was just a warm body he wanted to get closer to. "You mean I have short, dark hair."

"You're built like a dancer," he said. "I like that."

"Please go away."

"Feisty. I like that, too."

Before I should shoot him down for good, the dining-room door swung wide. In strolled a bulky middle-aged woman and a delicate grey-haired man. Benita greeted them and the man answered her so quietly I couldn't hear a word. Benita waved her hand toward the table and I made out the word Americanos. The big woman leaned down to whisper in the man's ear and he suddenly lit up, his cheeks pushing his oversized glasses up and his thin lips revealing yellowish teeth. "Why, you're Americans, too. That's just fabulous. Makes us feel at home already," he said.

"I'm Brian Lucas. Good to meet you. You folks watch TV? I was on 'All Our Tomorrows'."

"Well, you certainly do look familiar. I guess that's why. A star in our midst, how about that, honey?" The grey man sat down opposite me, his eyes owlishly huge behind his Coke-bottle glasses. The frames were grey, like his hair and clothing. He was the first person I'd seen in a suit since I'd left La Serena. The woman sat next to him, facing the soap-opera star. Up close, she was ghostly pale, with dyed-black hair and dark, baggy clothing. She took me in with a furtive glance and lowered her gaze to the table.

"This is Audrey," Brian said.

"I'm Ted and this is my wife, Mavis. Where are you from?"

"Los Angeles. Well, Oregon, originally, but L.A. now," Brian answered.

"What about you, Audrey?" Ted asked.

"New York."

"Wow, New York City?" Ted looked impressed. "I've always wanted to go there. But nobody's from the Big Apple, right? I mean, everyone's born somewhere else?"

I wondered if he recognized my face, if he was one of the tragedy vultures who circled around tragedies. "Born and bred there," I lied.

Ted gave a low whistle of appreciation. "We're from Kansas. I can't believe how long it took us to get here." He pushed his glasses back on his nose. "But, golly, it's worth it. We are just loving this beautiful country."

His wife nodded absently and stared into the distance. There was a wide window that overlooked the veranda and the well-groomed courtyard. It was October, which meant it was spring in Chile. Flowers bloomed around the hacienda, a fuchsia riot.

"It's the prettiest place I've ever seen. Don't you think so?" asked Ted.

"This your first time here?" Brian asked.

"First time ever out of the U S of A," Ted replied, as if there were any doubt.

"How'd you get here?" Brian asked.

"We flew?" Ted looked like he didn't understand the question.

"To this place, I mean. The guy who picked me up at the airport this morning should've picked you up, too."

"Oh, we rented a vehicle," Ted smiled.

"You drove here?" Brian was stunned. "Those roads are insane."

Ted was unperturbed. "Really? I thought it was a pretty."

"I can't believe you drove," Brian said. "I thought we'd fall off a cliff. I swear, every time I saw one of those roadside crosses, I wanted to get down on my knees and pray. Each one marks the scene of an accident where someone died."

My fork fell out of my hand. Brian didn't notice, but Ted and Mavis did.

"There are, like, dozens of them," Brian went on. "I thought driving in L.A. was crazy, but that's nothing. Here, a road is just a dirt path on the side of a mountain with no guardrail. You're taking your life in your hands."

I pushed my plate away. "I should be going. I'm running late." I knew how stupid that sounded. The hacienda was in the middle of nowhere. There was a tiny town maybe three miles away, and the hills were filled with goats. There was nothing to do except sit in the courtyard, hike the hills, or ride a horse. There were no televisions or phones in the guestrooms. There wasn't even a cell phone signal in the area. It was why I'd chosen the place.

Ted smiled at me. "See you later, alligator."

I made my escape. When I got back to my room, I threw up.

❖

Later that afternoon, I snuck out of the compound when I heard Brian's voice booming into the communal phone next to the dining room. I didn't want any company, especially not his.

I followed a twisting trail that led up from the valley. The trees and grasses gave way to scrub brush and cactus the higher I climbed. The sky was brilliant blue and dotted with puffy white clouds so evenly spaced that Magritte could have painted them. I got lost staring at it, remembering all the things I wanted to forget. By the time I came myself, the sun was drooping behind the mountains. I thought about staying out there, but I knew Benita and Miguel would send out a search party if I weren't back for dinner.

I got to the dining room five minutes after eight. The only empty seat was next to Brian, of course. He'd put on a white shirt that showed off his tan and rolled up the sleeves to reveal his biceps. "Hey, Audrey," he called, standing up to pull out my chair. Now that there were eight of us at the table, it felt crowded. The conversation that night was mostly in English since the American contingent was growing, and the German couple, Karl and Anke, spoke the language, too. Brian's baritone dominated the conversation. He gave us a blow-by-blow description of the complicated life of his soap-opera doppelganger. He'd been murdered a couple of months ago.

"What a surprise," I muttered, but Brian caught it.

"Don't worry," he said. "They can always bring me back as my evil twin."

By the time the cook carried out a dessert flan smothered in dulce de leche, conversation had turned to travel. Karl and Anke had been just about everywhere. "Why did you decide to come back here?" asked Ted.

"It's such a special, wonderful place," said Anke. "So distant from the outside world."

"Oh, that's what I like too," said Ted. "What are the people like around here?"

"Very kind, very helpful," said Anke. "Though we do spend most of our time with the horses."

"There was that time, we went up the mountain and I got dizzy. Is that the word, dizzy?" said Karl. "A goat herder came along and brought us back to his house. Very good people."

"Nice," Ted said. "Hey, Benita, you have any photos of your kids?"

Benita left the table, returning moments later with a hefty photo album. Her daughter was at school in Santiago. Her son worked for a winery in the Casablanca valley, an hour from the capital city.

"Such a lovely family," said Ted.

"Didn't the cook say something about her daughter?" Mavis asked.

Benita called to our cook, who came to the table with three dog-eared photographs.

"All girls?" asked Ted. "How wonderful."

The cook said something in rapid-fire Spanish. Karl translated for us. "Her eldest daughter will go high school in Santiago next year. Excellent student, she says."

I looked at the snapshots. The youngest of the cook's three daughters was seven or eight. The eldest was fourteen, beatific even in her navy school uniform and a small silver cross at her throat. I thought about my daughters, realizing Alison would have been ten and Caitlin would have been twelve now, if they had lived.

I tried to smile. "They're very pretty," I said. "Muy bonita." The cook beamed at me.

"Don't encourage them," Brian stage-whispered. "They'll bring out a slideshow."

Brian's one virtue, I realized, was that he made me angry. Around him, there was no room for sorrow and tears. I elbowed him and noticed Mavis watching us. She hadn't spoken a word during dinner, except to occasionally whisper in Ted's ear.

"Are you having a good time here, Mavis?" I asked.

"Oh, yes." Her eyes met mine. "You and your husband like it, don't you?"

For a moment I couldn't breathe. My husband's face floated past my eyes.

"We're not married. But it feels like we've known each other forever." Brian snaked his arm around the back of my chair and touched the back of my neck. He'd done that once during dinner and I'd stabbed him with my fork.

"Oh, my. I just assumed. She is wearing a wedding ring," said Mavis. Her eyes were heavily made up, and the result was almost raccoon-like on that pasty face. She looked ridiculous and yet I sensed malice under the layers.

"Smart girl, you wear it when you travel?" said Karl. "Our daughter does the same. So no one hassles you."

"Only it doesn't always work," said Anke, giving Brian a sidelong glance.

The conversation went on around the table. I waited five minutes before excusing myself and escaping to my room. I'd carried C.S. Lewis's *A Grief Observed* with me from New York, but I hadn't tried to read it on the plane. I didn't want it with me at all, but my husband had exacted from me a horrible promise. *Don't do anything drastic until you read it, my sweet angel.* We both knew what he meant by drastic. Cracking it open, I read, "No one ever told me that grief felt so like fear." A fat tear sploshed onto the page. I set the book aside, curled up on the brown comforter, and stared at the orange walls.

Afterwards I washed my face, but my eyes stayed swollen and red. I pulled on a sweater and stepped outside. The guestrooms all opened to the veranda. I stood in front of my door and stared up at the sky, looking for the Southern Cross. I could see Scorpio in the sky, turned upside-down from the way I knew it. There was a thin sliver of the moon, lit up only along its bottom edge so that it looked like a smile suspended among the stars. Evan had hated the fact you couldn't see the stars from Manhattan, so we used to drive upstate to look at them.

"I was wondering when you'd come out."

I jumped at the voice. Brian had caught me by surprise again. I could see the red tip of his cigarette glowing in the courtyard. "Don't tell me you've been waiting for me."

"Why not? There's nothing else to do here."

"I'm just going to bed."

"That's what I was thinking about, too." He exhaled loudly. "Bed, I mean."

"I got what you meant. No thanks."

"We could go for a walk."

"If I wanted a walk, I'd go for one by myself," I said.

"No you wouldn't. Not with Los Invisibles around."

"What are you talking about?"

"I've traveled around Bolivia and Peru and Chile before. They say a pretty girl can't walk alone in the countryside, because Los Invisibles will snatch her up."

I couldn't tell from his voice, but I had the feeling that he was playing with my head. "I don't believe in ghosts," I said, even as my mind suddenly returned to the man I'd sat next to on the plane, fingering those old clippings of lost girls as he wheezed. I felt a wave of nausea and sadness. I grabbed the railing of the veranda to steady myself, grateful for the darkness.

"Too smart for ghosts," said Brian. "Too smart to watch TV. What does a brainy girl like you do for fun?" He took my silence as an invitation to continue. "We could talk for a while. I've got some vodka in my room. And I picked up some really great stuff in Bolivia. What you can buy there for a few dollars on the street is unbelievable. Really good and pure."

It was like being in college again, with drunken frat boys trying to seduce me with dope. This kind of creepiness I could deal with. "No thanks."

With my eyes adjusting to the dark, I could see him. The veranda put me above the courtyard by a couple of steps, giving me a slight advantage, height-wise, but I felt as if he were the one looming over me. "What did you come here for, Audrey?"

"Peace and quiet."

"What are you running away from?"

I shrugged, and then realized the uselessness of a gesture in the darkness.

"It wouldn't kill you to be friendly," he said, throwing his cigarette down and stomping it. "Sleep tight." His retreating steps echoed through the courtyard. I stood on the veranda and watched him enter his room, where he became a shadow moving restlessly back and forth in front of a thinly curtained window. I wondered if he was getting high, and if he would come back out. There was a vein of deep-rooted aggression underneath his friendly façade. I pulled open my door and ducked inside. I'd turned off the lights when I'd gone out, not wanting to lure bugs in, and I didn't turn them on now. There was no lock on my door. Benita and Miguel had both boasted that you didn't need them. It was so safe, they claimed, they left the keys in the ignition of their jeep. My only security was a small latch you could fasten when you were inside the room. I felt for it, hooked it, and stood behind the door. I heard a doorknob turning softly.

I stared out the window, expecting Brian. Instead, Ted and Mavis passed by. They walked along silently; I could barely make out the soft sound of their footfalls on the flagstones. They moved off, across the courtyard and away. I waited longer and then, still in the dark, kicked my suitcase sideways until it was in front of the door. I sat down on the bed, pulled the duvet around me, and stayed on guard against passing shadows.

Breakfast at the hacienda was a major production. The offerings were laid out on a sideboard in the dining room: a skillet full of scrambled eggs, fresh cornbread, slices of turkey and ham, fruit salad. I tossed a couple of things I didn't plan to eat onto a plate and sat at the empty table just as Karl and Anke came in. The cook brought out mugs of steaming coffee. Mavis arrived alone, filled a plate, and sat down at the far end of the table. She was wearing a wrinkled black T-shirt and slacks, but her face was heavily made up. Her pale skin was powdered, her brows were penciled in, and her eyes were ringed with kohl. Her painted rosebud-red mouth completed an almost doll-like effect, but for the purple half-moons under her eyes that concealer didn't begin to cover up.

"How was your walk last night?" I asked her.

"What walk?" Mavis glanced at me quickly before returning her gaze to her plate.

"You and Ted were heading out when I was going to bed."

"Oh." She kept her eyes down. "I love looking at the stars."

That made my heart pound. Evan and I were both avid stargazers. We loved the stars so much we'd take our daughters out of the city to see them. That was why we were on the road the night a drunk driver in a truck smashed into our car. That was why our girls had died. Somehow, Evan and I had survived.

"You can see the center of the Milky Way on a clear night here," said Karl. "It looks like these funny clouds when you look straight up, but it's the stars clustered together."

"How do you find the Southern Cross?" I asked. Evan and I had, long ago, planned a stargazing trip to South America. It had never happened, but we'd talked about it before he died. My sweet angel, you can't leave this world without seeing the Southern Cross, he told me.

"I've seen it before, but not from here,'" said Karl. "I don't know if you can see it, with the mountains here."

"We went to Patagonia last year. You could see it well from there," added Anke.

"You can't see it from here?" I panicked. I'd daydreamed about dying on a starlit night, with my eyes on the constellation.

"You can only see it here for a few minutes around nine. It's too low on the horizon after that." Mavis's voice was low.

I made a mental note to look for it that night as Brian lumbered into the room. He looked haggard under his tan and tight T-shirt. "Where's the coffee?" he said, before heading toward the kitchen. As he passed me, I saw he was holding one of the photos the cook had shown us the night before.

"Where did you get that?" I asked him.

He shrugged. "It was outside. I guess the cook dropped it."

❖

The hacienda's routine was monotonous. Breakfast at eight, lunch at one, dinner at eight. In-between, you could go hiking or horseback riding. There was a sauna, but Benita or Miguel had to heat the room up in advance to use it. There were a couple of outlook points that you could reach on stairs leading down from the courtyard. One set took you almost to the river in the valley. The other, I'd already discovered, had a hammock and a couple of chairs. There were no stairs down from this lookout, just a sheer drop into the valley.

There was nothing to do and no one to talk to, which was what I'd thought I wanted. I was sick of hearing words of comfort that left me cold and desolate. *At least Evan isn't suffering anymore. He's in a better place. He's with your girls now.* I'd made the mistake of answering *Like hell* once, and my relatives muttered about it darkly. Brian had asked what I was running away from, which was surprisingly perceptive for a muscle-bound creep. I wondered if I'd scare him off by telling him the truth. I am a widow. My husband was my college sweetheart, and he died a long, agonizing death from cancer. But first, we were in a car accident that took our two little girls from us. My childhood faith is in the grave with them. Not that it mattered just then. Brian was off with Miguel for his first riding lesson. I headed down to the river. If I decided to go out Ophelia-style, this was my chance. No one was around to pull me back or hear me thrashing in the water. I wasn't exactly suicidal at that moment — I still had to read that book before I did anything drastic — but I liked having the option as a fallback plan.

Hilary Davidson

It turned out that the hacienda's river was barely a stream. I followed its banks, hoping that the real river would appear. The valley was green and leafy, and huge insects swooped by, but there was little else around except the occasional paddock with three or four horses. Most of the time I couldn't even see the river because of the trees along its bank. An hour into my walk I found a tree with a shiny new sign nailed to it. "No Trespassing!/No Traspase!" it declared. Before that, it hadn't occurred to me to wonder whose land I was on. Suddenly, I was curious. In for a penny, in for a pound, as Evan liked to say. The sign was posted next to what looked like a narrow corridor of trees. Seven steps in I came to a clearing. There was direct access to the little river at one end, and a couple of planks that extended partway over the water. There was a half-rolled sleeping bag at one end, and something silvery on the ground. I bent down to pick it up. It was a switchblade.

Little hairs stood up on the back of my neck. I looked around. There was no sign of anyone else. I set the knife down and stood. My mind was playing strange tricks on me. Maybe it was the pills I was taking. Maybe it was just bad luck that I'd sat next to a man obsessed with stories of missing girls, and then I'd heard the Los Invisibles story from Brian. It shook something inside me, and it made me want to crawl back into my room and not come out.

Instead, I waited there, but no one came by. Finally, as the sun went down, I made my way back to the house. In the courtyard, I bumped into Ted.

"Hey, there, Audrey," he said with a smile. He was carrying a large black case.

"Are you leaving?"

"Oh, no, not yet." He glanced at the case. "Just my gear."

"Your gear?" I remembered what Mavis had said. "For watching the stars?"

"That's right."

"Oh, was that your sleeping bag by the water?" I asked, finally putting two and two together. "Is that a spot you staked out for a telescope?"

He considered me silently for a moment. "It's supposed to be private." His voice wasn't so friendly now.

"I don't want to intrude. Mavis and I were talking about astronomy this morning. She told me you can only see the Southern Cross around nine."

Ted stared at me for a moment, before saying, "Funny you're so interested in the stars after what happened to your family."

His words hit me like a punch to the solar plexus. "What did you say?"

"Oh, sorry," Ted said, sounding more genial again. "Mavis remembered seeing a story about you on television. Maybe I shouldn't have brought it up. She said your family died in a car crash."

I swallowed hard. "My husband didn't. He died a month ago from a brain tumor." The words were bitter in my mouth. Evan knew he was dying long before the end came. He had time, not only to say goodbye, but to extract certain promises from me. He knew I wanted to end my own life, and he tried to trick me, right until the end, into going on living. *You still have a purpose in life, my sweet angel,* he claimed. I knew he was grasping at straws. How much tragedy was one person supposed to survive before cracking?

"Oh. How sad." There was a pause, filled with a commotion emanating from the dining room.

Ted started to say something else, but I brushed past him. "Excuse me."

Part of me wanted to run to my room, but the noise from the dining room was getting louder. I walked inside. The cook was screaming at Brian. Everyone else was watching, frozen.

"What's going on?"

"The cook's daughter is missing," Karl told me. "She thinks Brian had something to do with it."

"Why?"

"Because he had that photo of her daughter with him this morning," Karl said.

"And because of that joke he made about Los Invisibles," Anke added.

"I didn't do anything!" Brian said. "You're nuts, lady."

The cook went on yelling, waving her hands around boldly, before putting her hands over her eyes and dissolving in tears. Benita and Miguel moved closer to comfort her, while Karl and Anke gave Brian the evil eye.

"I didn't do anything," Brian said to me. He grabbed my arm and pulled me outside. "These people are crazy."

"Let go of me!" I demanded.

"Don't tell me you think I did something to her?" he asked, but he let go.

"Did you?"

"Of course not! What kind of question is that?" He shook his head. "I think this place is making everyone crazy."

"You seem to be the nutty one."

"Oh, yeah? Everyone's jumping on me for cracking a joke about Los Invisibles. You know what? That German couple have been to South America several times, visiting Peru and Bolivia and Chile — all the places where girls have gone missing."

"You've been to all those places, haven't you?" I asked. "Maybe you're Los Invisibles. What were you doing with that photo this morning?"

"Nothing! I found it under my door this morning."

I stared at him. "You expect anyone to believe that? You've got the girl's photo, and then she goes missing? You don't see anything weird about that?"

"No, I don't."

"This morning, you said you found the photo outside," I pointed out. "Now, you say it was under your door. Which is the truth?"

"It was under my door." His voice was low. "I thought that was weird, so I said I found it outside."

I stared at him, shaking my head. Then I turned and walked away from him, heading for my room. I could hear his footsteps echoing behind me. I opened the door to my room and closed it quickly. Just as I was about to latch it, someone grabbed me in the dark.

"This is what you get for meddling," Ted said.

I felt I cold piece of metal touch my neck. But my door flew open, hitting us and knocking me off balance.

"Look, I shouldn't have joked about Los Invisibles..." Brian said, switching on the light. Then he saw Ted. "What are you doing in Audrey's room?"

Ted's thin lips formed a perfect O. "Oh, I wasn't... I mean, I didn't... Oh my goodness, I know it's late. I should be going." He moved past me but was blocked by Brian, whose body filled the doorway.

"He grabbed me," I said. "I think he was going to kill me."

"Don't me silly," Ted said. "I was just..."

I saw Ted's right hand come out of his pocket and a flash of silver as he struck Brian. A seam of red opened on Brian's cheek, his neck, and across his chest. He fell forward and Ted ran out the door.

Brian looked at his chest and raised a hand to his face. "Did that little creep just stab me?" He slumped to the floor.

"Help!" I screamed, running out of the room. "Brian's been stabbed!"

I kept screaming until people came running. Benita and Miguel and the German couple hurried to help. An engine revved, and I ran around the veranda to the far side of the hacienda, where the parking lot was. Mavis was behind the wheel of a black SUV, and Ted was clambering inside. There was a moment where I locked eyes with her, and the second Ted shut his door, she tore out of the spot and pointed the vehicle at me.

I'm going to die, I thought. I'd come to this very spot to kill myself, but now that someone else was eager to do the job for me, I didn't want to go. I threw myself back onto the veranda and scrambled across the boards as Mavis rammed the corner of the house. The impact broke a few boards, but the house was on a stone foundation that didn't budge. Mavis reversed and hit it again, then pulled the vehicle around and raced out of the little lot and onto the road.

I ran to the hacienda's white jeep. The door was unlocked and the keys were in the ignition, just like Benita had said. In such a low-crime area, who bothered with security? I tore out of the lot in pursuit.

In hindsight, things got clearer. When Ted and Mavis had arrived at the hacienda, I'd thought they were wearing costumes. Mavis's makeup was ridiculous. But I saw now that it was camouflage. They painted themselves as ignorant travelers, and we'd taken them at their word. We should have realized that no first-time visitors to the area took on the crazy, dangerous drive from the airport.

It was hard to catch up with Mavis and Ted, but no challenge to find them. There were no other roads that connected with the one we were on, not for a long while. I caught sight of their SUV a couple of times, winding around the mountain as lightning speed. The road climbed around a hill, and I stepped on the gas. On the right was a sheer, steep drop. It was dark, but the sky was clear and filled with stars. A faint, glimmering light caught on a little shrine around a curve. Someone had died in this spot. Seeing it, I realized what I was going to do. I didn't care about danger, only about stopping them.

Swooping around another curve, I sped up and rammed the black SUV with the jeep. The wheels on the right tipped over the ledge, stopping the vehicle dead even though the wheels on the right were spinning. The empty night air was filled with their screeching.

Mavis opened the door on the driver's side and hopped out. Ted was yelling at her. He screamed, "What are you doing?" as he clambered over to the driver's side to escape the vehicle. But Mavis was too fast for him. She slammed the door, and the precariously perched SUV tipped to the right and hurtled down. By the time I got out of the jeep and looked over the cliff, it was on fire.

"Ted made me do it," Mavis said. "I didn't have a choice. It was Ted. It was all Ted."

"Nice attempt at framing Brian," I said. "Putting a photo of your victim under his door."

"That guy's a creep," Mavis spoke without a trace of irony. "Anyway, that was Ted's idea."

"Why go hunting in this region?"

"Ted spent a high-school semester in Chile back when Augusto Pinochet was still in power. He said people disappeared all the time." She stared at the fire below. "It's so much easier to fool the authorities here than at home."

"Is the cook's daughter still alive?"

"Yes. We... Ted was going to have his fun with her tonight, then make her disappear."

"Where is she now?"

After Mavis told me, I shoved her off the cliff. The look of shock on her pale face as she went down was priceless. I stood on the edge, aware that, barely an hour ago, I would have happily jumped into the abyss. But I didn't want to anymore. I had to return to the hacienda and save the girl. And that wouldn't be the end of the story.

As I drove the jeep back to the hacienda, I spotted the Southern Cross for the first time. I could almost hear Evan's voice. Those explorers in the southern hemisphere had it rough, he'd told me. All the northerners had to do was follow the North Star. Measure from the head to the foot, go four-and-a-half times that distance to the left, and that's the pole. The Southern Cross wasn't as easy a guide at the North Star, but it was just as true.

As the jeep swooped around the mountain road, I watched the Southern Cross disappear below the horizon. I was alone with a sky of strange stars. That didn't bother me anymore. The fear and loneliness I'd known so intimately was gone. I realized my husband had been right all along. I hadn't been able to save my own daughters, but I could help other lost girls. I had found my purpose.

ABOUT THE AUTHOR

Hilary Davidson was a journalist before she turned to the dark side and started writing crime fiction. Her novels include the award-winning Lily Moore series—*The Damage Done, The Next One to Fall,* and *Evil in All Its Disguises*—the bestselling Shadows of New York series—*One Small Sacrifice* and *Don't Look Down*—and the standalone novels *Blood Always Tells* and *Her Last Breath*. She is also the author of some fifty short stories. Her fiction has won two Anthony Awards, a Derringer Award, and a host of other accolades. Her novels have been translated into French, German, Hungarian, Polish, Romanian, and Russian. Toronto born and raised, she moved to New York City in October 2001. She is also the author of eighteen nonfiction books.

Her next novel, *Every Lie I Told,* will be published by Blackstone in June 2026.

www.ingramcontent.com/pod-product-compliance
Lightning Source LLC
Chambersburg PA
CBHW030821020726
47499CB00006B/2020